Year of the Dogman

FRANK HOLES, JR

YEAR OF THE DOGMAN

2007

Year of the Dogman

ACKNOWLEDGEMENTS

A novel of this magnitude, which is based on both fictional accounts and actual sightings and encounters by the good folks of Michigan over many years, requires the assistance of many people. My deepest thanks go out to the following professionals who have aided the success of this novel: Craig Tollenaar, cover artist extraordinaire, who designed the book cover and all of our marketing materials; Sergeant Todd Woods, Mackinaw City Police Department, for his help with the technical details regarding law enforcement; Eli Holes, my grandfather, who diligently read, re-read, proofread, and edited the first editions; the crew over at BookSurge who have made the publishing process a fun and exciting ride; and Steve Cook, Traverse City DJ and creator of the song "The Legend" which was my initial inspiration for this novel.

The novel that follows is a work of fiction. Although the many towns and cities surrounding Twin Lakes are real places, the village itself exists completely in the mind of the author. Any resemblance between the folks who live there and people who live in the real world is coincidental and unintended.

The Dogman, however, is very real to those who have seen or encountered the beast. Take a long walk outside in the north woods in the depths of the night if you don't believe me.

Official *Year of the Dogman* information and merchandise can be found at our website:

http://www.dogman07.com

To My Wife Michele,
My Son James,
And To All Of My Students, Past And Present.

The Dogman Is Real.

It's Important To Believe...

CHAPTER 1

Prologue: October 1707

The two long, white, birch-bark canoes slipped through the river, making hardly a sound. They were highly maneuverable, and would glide forward both down and up river with the easiest of strokes. Each river craft rode lightly in the rippling water, its wide beams effortlessly distributing the weight of paddlers and the mounds of stored gear, which could easily be over 800 pounds. Stability was guaranteed both on river and lake, on still or rushing water. Their great size enabled them to carry huge loads, making the most of any trip. They were often weighed down with supplies and goods before trading, and they rode even lower on the trip back, stuffed to the gunwales with furs. And yet with all that weight, each craft's 20-foot length was as nimble as a swimmer in open water.

The four paddlers, three experienced French trappers and their dark-skinned Algonquin guide, steered a course up a small, winding tributary of the O-Wash-Ta-Nong River. The O-Wash-Ta-Nong was easily the largest river in the Michigana land, heading east and southeast from its 80-foot-wide mouth at the great western lake of the territory to its sparkling headwaters nearly 300 miles inland. The fur traders had already made three stops at Ottawa villages on the banks of this river, trading for the valuable mink, beaver, raccoon, and other small game furs, as they made their two-week-long trek up and then back down the river.

In the early 1700s, such furs were the currency in France's little civilization carved out of the new world wilderness. Hundreds of trappers and traders, novices and experts, went out into the untamed wild in their birch-bark canoes to trade trinkets, muskets, various pieces of hardware, and tobacco and whiskey to the indigenous peoples for the furs that were all the fashion rage in the old world. Furs in the new world served far more useful purposes than those sent over the Atlantic. Settlers and explorers alike used the furs for making everything from pouches to clothing to blankets.

Jacques, steering the back canoe, was a huge bulk of a man, his six-foot-four frame easily towering over his fellow companions even when he sat in a water craft. Warmly dressed in a plaid red flannel and thick leather boots for the unexpected weather conditions of the Michigana land, his long black curly beard completed the appearance of a man of the wilderness. In front of him, his partner Francois pulled his oar effortlessly through the water with his muscular, beefy arms. He was much shorter than his companion, only about five-foot-two, but he had a barrel of a chest and short but thick arms and legs, which were covered with a coarse blanket of hair. The stubble of his black beard stood in contrast to the tanned deerskin leather jacket and pants he wore year-round. Despite his appearance as a squared-off block of granite, Francois was always in a good mood, his face ready to spread in a great smile as he observed the beauty of the natural world around him. The land never failed to impress and delight him.

The first canoe was paddled from the front by Pierre, also short compared to Jacques the giant. He wore a dark green stocking hat topping off curly, stringy hair that reached down to his neckline. A long, wispy moustache curled up around his cheeks from the top of his upper lip. His green suspenders held up his wool trousers that overlapped his outdoor shirt jacket. Pierre was the quiet one of the group, often lost in his own thoughts. The others accepted this, as they told stories and sang all day long and each evening around the campfires they lit for cooking.

And steering Pierre's canoe was their Algonquin guide, Etchemin, who dressed much lighter than the three white men, wearing a light shirt and deerskin shorts. A veteran of many trips into the middle of the Michigana land, Etchemin knew the weather and climate well and took as little as he could on each trip. Like Pierre, Etchemin said very little, but he did narrate and interpret the various interesting land features to the Frenchmen.

The four had worked out of the log-stockade fort at the straits of Mackinac this entire year, paddling up the many rivers all around the great Michigana, and they would return there a few weeks later when all of their goods had been traded for the valuable furs. The fort and settlement at Mackinac was an okay place to spend the frigid winter, but they wished they could push on and return home to Montreal before the winter ice thawed. The little settlement at the tip of Michigana's peninsula was the home to several hundred settlers, explorers and fur trappers, and it did have some of the comforts those in the wilderness enjoyed. But of course, there was nothing quite like the comforts of home.

Even Etchemin, who had traveled all over this land over the course of many years, wanted to return to his people back in the east. He was chosen for this trip because of his fluency in French and the several languages spoken by tribes in Michigana land, as well as his familiarity with the country and his skilled handling of canoes. And he was an expert on the water. He had spent the previous four years in and around the region, leading numerous trading trips and expeditions for the French traders and explorers. Money was not a motivating factor for Etchemin, though he was paid well for his services. He, like many of his ancestors, enjoyed the adventure of living as one with the wilderness. It was the way the Great Spirit had intended his people to live in their youth. When his people eventually became older, they would then settle down in the villages, raising children who would one day set off on their own into the wild like their fathers had done a generation earlier.

This last trip of the autumn season began several weeks earlier when the four traders left the wilderness fort at the northernmost point of this land and paddled their way south along Lake Michigana, or the *Great Water*, as the natives called it. Looking out across the Great Water, one had a hard time telling it was a lake. It was so huge it might have been a sea or even an ocean, for all anyone knew. Only the explorers who'd been there knew there was an opposite shore many miles in the distance. The four fur traders kept close to the shoreline to avoid the huge swells of the lake, and yet deep enough not to bottom out. For most of the trip, the water was a deep blue, reflecting the nearly cloudless sky. Few small waves lapped up lazily onto the sandy beaches lining the shoreline. But it was a deceiving façade.

The season's great storms had yet to fully develop, but Jacques knew they would very soon, and their fury would be magnificent. There was nothing like an early-winter storm that had the time to fully brew up over the great lakes and then bombard the land with all the ferocity nature could muster. Jacques knew the storm season was quickly approaching, and he wanted to finish up this last trip and return before it hit. Even now they were on borrowed time. A storm now before the cold temperatures froze the rivers and lakes of this land could still be fatal if they were caught in it. Being a trader in the wilderness carried with it certain risks to life and limb, but Jacques also didn't want to tempt fate. He'd just as soon finish their business here and return to the safety of the fort.

After first traveling up the Manistee River and trading with two villages, and then paddling up the Muskegon River, trading with two more villages, this small group of traders continued south to their final river cruise. They had done fairly well up both rivers, and a little more than half of their goods had been traded for furs by the time they reached the mouth of the O-Wash-Ta-Nong River.

The last stop on their voyage, this particular Ottawa village was situated on the banks of a small tributary about half a day's journey up from O-Wash-Ta-Nong River. The tributary, really just a large creek only a few feet deep, led into a wooded valley, the trees already beginning their change from basic green leaves to the brilliant reds, yellows, and oranges of the fall color season. This village was unique, Etchemin told the Frenchmen, because the high chief of this region was situated there. This chief gave direction to the entire Ottawa tribe spread over the land. It would be an excellent place to trade for furs and share information.

The cries of several lookouts welcomed the traders to the village. The canoes rounded a bend in the river and saw the river split around an unusual, grassy high mound surrounded by a smaller ledge of raised earth and flat, chipped stone slabs. Nothing like it had ever been seen by the Frenchmen. The traders took the larger and deeper fork to the right of the strange mound. Scantily clad children and young men jumped up and down and ran along the bank opposite the strange mound leading them to the village. They were obviously excited to see the trappers, and their cries let the entire valley know the Frenchmen had arrived.

When the long canoes beached on the muddy creek bank, the traders noticed that the grassy mound was actually an island right in the middle of the creek. The island was probably 80 feet long, but the height of the mound, probably a dozen feet tall, kept them from telling how far it was across to the opposite bank. However, their sightseeing was soon distracted by the many natives crowding around them.

They were welcomed like honored guests. Their guide had been up this tributary before, and he exchanged greetings with the members of the tribe he hadn't seen in a long time. The traders were escorted to the center of the little village where families began bringing out all sorts of items to trade. There were furs of all kinds, along with delicious foods, tools, and weapons, hand made from bones, and of course the little trinkets created by the local artisans.

The village was far from a permanent settlement. The small, dark lodges were hand-crafted from flexible tree branches lashed together and covered with overlapping hides. Standing about seven feet tall and perhaps 20 feet in diameter, each had a central door opening to the center of the village, and the great tribal fire pit, which was encircled by large rounded stones. Smaller cooking fires were situated in between several lodges, obviously forming tight family groups, and the delicious smells from these were heavenly to the travelers who had eaten dried meat and pemmican for several weeks. The members of the tribe who had not stopped to trade continued on their daily tasks of cooking, cleaning skins, and building or repairing vital structures in the village while the children ran about playing games.

Pleasantries over, it was time for business. The trading began right away. The Frenchmen dickered patiently with the natives, offering metal pots and pans, a few small pistols and ammunition, rolled tobacco, small bottles of whiskey, pouches of sugar, and other delicacies from the sophisticated world for the various furs. In some ways, it almost seemed unfair, giving away the staples of civilized life for the skins of animals that were killed in the wilderness. But the fur business was astonishing. These skins, plentiful here in the backwoods, were the currency of the new world, and were even fought over back in Europe.

A few hours later, the business was done, and the traders were pleased with their efforts and bartering. They packed up the bundles of furs tightly and stowed them under their canoes, which were turned over in case of rain.

The day faded into the dim twilight, the last of the sun's rays setting down below the tree tops and shining through the leaves, illuminating the brilliant yellows, oranges, and reds. A light breeze shook them, and the entire forest took on the look of a rippling meadow of colorful flowers. The beauty of the autumn was never lost on the Frenchmen, nor on their guide. Despite the inevitable storms, and the danger of traveling in the late fall, they absolutely loved this time of year.

At the village fire that evening, the four guests were treated like kings. They feasted for hours on succulent venison, roasted game bird, and fish. A light and crumbly form of cornbread pancake was baked over the fire on flat, hot rocks and eaten with berries and nuts. It was delicious. Afterwards, they were presented with small tokens proclaiming them friends of the tribe. And after the remnants of daylight finally slipped into the darkness of night, the traders were invited to smoke with the head men of each family, including the high chief, Gray

Elk. When all were relaxed, recovering from the massive feast, the storytelling began. Several men of the village told stories about the happenings in the valley, the preparations the tribe would make for the coming winter months, and the various exploits of the youth in the village. Many laughed merrily over these stories, remembering their own adventures in years past. The Frenchmen were asked for news from the other villages they'd visited, and each of the three shared stories of the lands they had visited on their many trips. Finally, as the black night completely closed over the valley, Jacques asked the question the traders had been pondering since they arrived.

"The great mound on the island in the river is very interesting. What is it?" he asked the village men.

One old family head held up his wrinkled hands, palms outward, in a negative gesture and started, "We do not speak of the dead hill," but he was interrupted by the high chief.

"The white men have shared tales with us this evening," Chief Gray Elk stated. "And they are as our brothers. They have shared council with us this night. It is only right that we share with them."

"I meant no insult, great chief," Jacques said respectfully, bowing his head, knowing he might be on shaky ground. "The great mound is hard to miss. We've not seen anything like it in our many journeys. We just wondered what it was."

The chief stared into the glowing fire embers for a long time, and then closed his eyes. His eyebrows furrowed for a few moments, the lines of his leathery face wrinkled up. That instant he looked decades older, as if he had aged there on the spot. Then his face lightened up, and he relaxed and was peaceful again. He opened his eyes, took a long puff from his carved pipe, and stared through the delicate fingers of fire at the white men seated across from him.

Chief Gray Elk began: "It has been a long time, my friend, since we talk of these things. It is usually enough that we tell our children so they stay away from the dead hills. We do not speak of them ourselves. They are places of evil, and we stay away. The white men do not know, they do not ask, and so we do not tell. You are the first to ask, and the first white men to know the story."

Jacques then remembered that despite all the children who had run along the creek to greet them on the way in, all were on the same side as the village. Not a single person had been on the banks of the little island. The Chief was right; no one, not even the children, had set foot on the island in the middle of the creek.

"In ancient times, tribes from the south, the Yam-Ko-Desh, invaded our territory. They were an evil people, and they could not live in peace with anyone. These 'prairie people' believed they had the right to rule the world. They brought with them their families, and their gold and jewels, which they prized above all. We care nothing for gold and jewels. They have no meaning for us, and they are not useful.

"The Yam-Ko-Desh attacked our villages, killed our people. They ate the flesh of those they killed, and they worshipped a god with a wolf's head. Their warriors wore the skins and heads of the wolf, and they believed they became one with the wolf when in battle. It gave them great strength and courage. No tribe had withstood them.

"Our ancestors knew they could not stop them alone. So they joined with our neighbors the Ojibwa and the Potawatomie, and together the three tribes defeated the Yam-Ko-Desh, the 'prairie people.' Our ancestors buried their remains in the great hills of the dead you see on the island. All of their cursed weapons, tools, gold and jewels, and the totems of their wolf cult were buried with them. Our medicine men placed spells over the dead hills and asked the Great Spirit to keep the evil buried forever.

"Before the evil people came to these lands, our three tribes wanted nothing to do with each other. We were not at war, but we were not always peaceful. After we drove away the Yam-Ko-Desh, we united as the Three Fires. Our chiefs, our people, became friends and allies. We promised to always protect the lands of the Great Spirit and our people. This peace has lasted for a long time. I hope it continues for a long time to come."

The men around the fire sat silently for a time, thinking about the story they'd just heard. Though the tale was not new to the Ottawa, the native men were silently lost in deep thoughts of the past. The three white men had never heard anything like it. The chief noticed this, and said, "I see from your faces you have more questions to ask me. I will answer with all that I know."

"So what are those small ledges around the dead hills?" asked Francois, obviously intrigued. "Why are the rocks so jagged?"

The Chief pulled from his pipe for a long second, exhaling the opaque smoke into the dark folds of the night before answering the Frenchman. He gazed, unblinking, through the bright fire. "The bones of our long dead warriors guard the evil spirits from escaping. The edges of the garden beds are sharp and angular, and they change direction so even if the ghosts of the Yam-Ko-Desh rose from the earth, they could not find their way out before the spirits of their captors stopped them."

"Why were the dead hills put on an island, of all places?" Jacques asked.

"I know nothing of the spirits of the white men, but the ghosts of our people cannot cross running water," the Chief answered. "Unless they are helped across, the island makes a final prison of the dead hills. Unless released, the evil of the Yam-Ko-Desh will never rise again."

A great hush fell over the gathering around the council fire. Each man, white and red, was lost in his own thoughts. Jacques was thinking of his own ancestry back in France, his family who had never wanted anything to do with the new world. They'd basically disowned him, and that was fine with him. He'd come to the new world to explore, to carve a piece of the wilderness for his own, to escape the irritating, overcrowded and highly political society. He was free here. Though he represented his king and country, he was his own man here, making his own choices and his own name for himself.

Thoughts of his beautiful, young fiancée back in Montreal occupied Francois. They were still a few months from returning home, and the two would be married when he came back. The compensation from this trip would pay for their first home, and he'd make them a good life. They were simple folks, and they didn't need any riches or frills. Perhaps this would even be his last trip into the wilderness. Of course he enjoyed the wild, but he could get used to settling down, sharing stories with his children around their hearth. He'd do all he could to make this a profitable trip, and then enjoy a new lifestyle with his new family.

Pierre was looking past the fire into the still darkness, listening to the whisper of the little tributary of the O-Wash-Ta-Nong River. He was drawn to money, like a moth to a candle. Though he couldn't see the great mound, he knew it was there only a bit across the little creek. A wealth of gold and jewels was just waiting there, a mere hundred feet away, for him to help himself. These natives didn't want them; they said themselves they had no interest in them. He could dig them up in no time and really make this trip more than worthwhile. Unlike Jacques and Francois, Pierre was in the new world to build a fortune. Plenty of his countrymen had found their fortunes. This was his golden opportunity, and he'd certainly not let some silly old superstition stop him.

A loud, shrill cry went out behind the seated men, and several among the fire jumped. But it was only a pair of young warriors starting a dance. They howled out at each other in some tribal time-honored tradition. But the smiles on their faces let the Frenchmen know this was the beginning of the entertainment. A large tribal drum began a steady, throbbing beat. Soon the entire tribe was singing along as more of the Ottawa joined in the dancing. Even the Frenchmen and their guide were tugged along by the young women and the children, until everyone was enjoying the evening. Everyone, that is, except for Pierre, who sat off to the side of the fire, lost in his thoughts and plans for the future, both long-term and immediate.

***

Late that evening, a furtive, dark shadow moved through the camp, carefully treading around the lodges, stealing ever closer to the river. The full moon, silvery-white and directly overhead, enabled the man to see the ground with full clarity, avoiding anything that could make a noise and might give him away. The camp was fully asleep after the evening's reverie, and the shadow man knew this was his one chance. He carefully stepped through the river, doing his best to avoid any splashing. He came up dripping from his knees down onto the bank of the island and approached the dead hill. It loomed over him, even in the darkness. It was easily higher than he was tall, and was easily longer than four canoes stretched end to end. The moon shone off the thick grass covering the mound, and it surprised Pierre that nothing else grew on it. All around the hill was the garden bed, edged by stacked, jagged rocks. The garden bed was a giant's step up to the dead hill, and it was covered with small shrubs that were ordinarily very colorful in the sunlight. They were a contrast to the dead hill itself, though Pierre didn't appreciate it, or even notice it. His mind was concentrated on the task at hand.

He moved forward, little shovel in hand, and stepped up onto the rocky ledge of the garden-bed. At that moment, the north woods wind kicked up, cooling his wet legs and sending shivers up his back. He paused for a moment as a long, low howl passed through the valley. A lone wolf was crying far off in the distance. Pierre obviously knew the sounds of the wilderness, and they did nothing to spook him. He'd spent many years of his life exploring, trapping and trading on the frontier, and there was little in the forest that scared him. Two strides brought him to the base of the great mound. But at that point, he did stop for a moment. Something didn't feel right to him. It was nothing he could hear, see, or smell, but it was more of a feeling, a sense. A word passed through his mind, *trespasser.* Where did that come from? He shook his head, his stringy hair drifting in the breeze, and reminded himself why he was there. This was his fortune to find, his chance at a life of luxury. He strode up the mound to its very top. It gave him a wonderful black and white view of the valley floor, the river, the camp stretching up into the forest all around.

Pierre raised his shovel, and drove it forcefully into the soft earth. The loose soil gave easily, and soon he had excavated a fairly sizable hole. The moon rose high overhead, bathing the entire area in its glow, lighting up the mound just like it was day. Pierre had no problem seeing the small artifacts his shovel brought to the surface. At first there were small, uninteresting tools, arrowheads, and pottery. Then he found the necklace. He dropped to his knees at the edge of the hole and brushed away the dirt from the jewelry. Even after being buried in the earth for untold years, the jewels glistened in the moonlight. The Frenchman brought it up to his eyes, rubbed the dark jewels between his fingers while blowing the remaining dirt specks from them. Ah, an excellent find! Each of the two dozen or so jewels laced along the rawhide thong was triangular in shape, sharpened down nearly to a keen point. They almost resembled the claws, or possibly the fangs, of an animal. Probably a totem necklace belonging to a warrior, the Frenchman thought. A dog-warrior, perhaps. The old chief had mentioned that in his story. But there was undoubtedly more, he thought as he lowered the necklace down over his head and around his long hair and neck, being careful to hide it beneath his over-shirt. It wouldn't do to have anyone see it. The necklace securely in place, he returned his attention to the excavation. He must keep digging.

After another shovel full of dirt and more treasures, the true excitement hit him. More jewelry, some interspaced with gold and shells, was unearthed. He filled his pouch with the promise of his soon-to-be-wealthy future. Pierre cast the shovel aside and began digging through the loose dirt with his hands. He lay right down on the earth, fingers sifting through the soil. His fingers felt something large, solid, and very firm. The anticipation of a large gem built up to a frenzy. This was it. This was what he came for. He pulled it out of the earth and sat back on his haunches. And in that moment, his excitement dissipated as his hands brought up to his face a human skull.

It was cracked at the back and sides where it was missing the jaw bone. A hole was nicely pierced on its forehead, above and between the eye sockets. This was the skull of a warrior who had died in battle, and the trauma to the bone was its testament. Pierre held the battered skull, eyes gazing into its empty sockets. He was drawn to it, into it. All other thoughts had left his mind.

Suddenly his hands began to tremble. He heard that word in his mind again, but this time he thought he heard it aloud also. *Trespasser.* The word wasn't in French, and he didn't recognize it as Ottawa, but he understood it nonetheless. The skull turned black, and darkness surrounded him as the moon slipped behind a cloud. A frigid blast of wind hit him full in the chest and face. A chill, a spasm, rocked his body. He dropped the skull back into the earth and fell over onto his back. The word blasted through his brain, stinging his senses. His eyes closed violently, and he grasped the sides of his head. *Trespasser.* He heard it once again, aloud for sure this time, and when he scrambled to leave, he realized it wasn't even in a language he'd ever heard before. It was a low snarl that built to a deep howl. A wolf's howl. He had heard and understood a wolf's howl. How could that be? And worse yet, it was right behind Pierre. He turned to face it as the moon escaped the cloud bank, and there he saw the largest wild dog he'd ever seen in his life. And yet, it was not quite a dog. That was the only thing his mind could remotely connect this creature to. It was covered in a dark, stringy fur, and its head was misshapen. It wasn't quite a normal canine shape, but there was nothing normal to really describe it. It glowed in the moonlight, a ghostly specter against the darkness of the woods.

The creature stood on the near bank of the creek, about 20 feet away, bright yellow slanted eyes glowing and staring unblinkingly at him. Its lips curled back, revealing deeply stained fangs dripping with saliva. It was easily four feet high at the top of its head. To the Frenchman's horror, it took a step forward and upward, pulling its body up into a human stance and moved forward slowly on its back two legs.

Pierre staggered back the way he originally came, but slipped into the hole he had dug. His ankles, wrists, and the back of his head kept him from completely falling in, though he lost his pouch of valuables, not that he noticed. He continued to scramble backward, facing the creature, but his feet were stuck in the dirt. The more he kicked to escape the hole, the farther he sank in. The earth was sucking him down! He pushed with his hands, his forearms, and twisted his body as the dirt pulled him down. He was buried up nearly to his knees already, and his panic overcame all senses. He'd forgotten the monster above and struggled to free himself from the grasp of the mound. He wanted to scream for help but no sound came from his throat.

Luck, or perhaps providence, finally came to Pierre as his left foot pushed off something solid, and he took full advantage of the moment, freeing his legs and pushing himself from the cavity. He scrambled backward, and then remembered the dog creature. He looked up to see it glaring down at him from across his hole. Its front legs were more like muscular arms, he saw now, large black claws clicking together as it flexed its hand/paw. He could smell the rotting flesh of its breath, and he felt nausea on top of everything else. He noticed the glow of its body was actually the moonlight shining through it. It was a ghostly apparition!

Pierre somehow knew if he could get to the river, he'd be safe. That was what the Chief had told them: the spirits couldn't cross the water. He kicked his feet out and tried to sprint for the water. He felt more than heard the demon launch itself across the hole and race him to the safety of the shore. Pierre struggled down the slope and his leather moccasins caught and tripped over the stone edge of the garden bed. His chin hit the ground first, followed by the rest of his body. Intense pain shot through his head from the impact, but he ignored it. He rolled over just in time to see the demon leap from the mound, arms and legs spread, claws elongated, jaws open wide in what looked like a savage grin. My god, he thought, could an animal actually grin? He heard its roar reverberate through his mind. The Frenchman closed his eyes, his hands up and over his face, teeth gritted in a futile attempt to save himself.

The impact was nothing that he expected. It was like a blast of wind that pressed his chest and body flat into the ground at the river bank. He felt an icy coldness spread through his body, right to the edge of his fingers, toes, and all extremities. The pressure stayed on top of him, clawed and pierced into his skin, and he refused to open his eyes and look at his attacker. He slipped into unconsciousness, hopeful that he wouldn't feel the inevitable pain of his death and dismemberment.

***

But he didn't die. He awoke on the bank of the creek and saw the mound across from him when he sat up. His fingers felt over his face, his neck, and his body. He carefully looked himself over to be sure he was still alive. Pierre couldn't believe he wasn't dead. He took several minutes to catch his breath. His heart was thumping in his chest, and his senses were alive. Then it hit him that he was looking across the creek at the mound he'd dug into earlier. The full moon's light still shone down below, but there were more shadows since it had moved across the sky. He must have been out for several hours. It would be morning soon, as the old familiar deep blue began to overcome the black in the east through the trees. How did he get back across the water? And why wasn't he filthy from the dirt and grime of digging? He looked carefully at his dig site, but he couldn't see any scar in the earth. It was as if he'd never been there. Had he dreamed the entire thing? No, he could remember the excavation, the find, and the creature. He shivered. He wished it had been only a nightmare, but his memory told him otherwise.

The only things that definitively told him it had really happened were the necklace under his shirt and his missing pouch. He yearned to go across the water to find where the pouch dropped, but it was far too close to morning, and undoubtedly some of the tribe would be awake with the early coming morn. With a regretful grimace from losing his fortune, he stole away from the creek and sneaked back to his bed roll before anyone could notice he'd left. He didn't know what any of the tribe would do if they found him here, or if they knew he'd been on the island. And after the events of the night, he didn't want to find out.

***

Well before mid-morning, the three Frenchmen and their guide packed up the massive load of furs, their packs and the re-supply of dried meats and stores into the large canoes. They bid their farewells to the Ottawa tribe, pushed off from the shore, canoes nearly dragging bottom, and set off toward the O-Wash-Ta-Nong and the great lake. Already the crisp autumn air was cooler than when they had arrived the previous day. The sky was overcast, the gray clouds blowing quickly over the world from the whipping wind. It was funny, Jacques thought, you could feel the change of seasons in just a day. He buttoned up his jacket around his neck and continued to paddle, aided by the current. There would be no singing today.

They joined back with the main river a few hours later, and the wind was kicking up mists of water that left little droplets on their clothing. Already they could see a storm on the rise. They quickened their pace, pushing on and making good time heading downstream. Afternoon brought the first of the rain, big heavy drops that streaked down their faces. But they did not stop. There was no cover anyway, and everything they carried would withstand even the heaviest of rainstorms if necessary. But the Frenchmen and their guide knew they couldn't last long on the great water of Michigana, especially if this storm was typical of the early winter tempests that built wildly one after another, sometimes for weeks at a time. They'd have to press on if they hoped to reach the fort at Mackinac before the storms brought deadly snow and ice.

Less than half an hour after the drops started, the heavens opened up and poured forth the torrents of rain. Again, they doubled their efforts, now aided by the rising water and the increased speed of the current. They quickly passed the previous two villages, but they were quiet, all the inhabitants safely inside, out of the storm. There was not even a thought of stopping; to do so might strand them for the winter, and they didn't want to overstay their welcome.

What took nine days to travel upstream only took two to return to the great lake, such was the force of the rushing water that carried them back. Along with the pounding rain came sharp gales of wind that snapped limbs and blew the leaves from the trees, bent the river grasses over and stung the skin. Unfortunately, the surge of the river moved opposite the wind gusts, making it very uncomfortable for the travelers.

Etchemin was abnormally quiet during the return. Through the rain, Jacques noticed him often looking deeply into the woods on either side of the river. Something was obviously troubling him. Jacques even tried in vain to see what the guide was staring at, looking carefully into the forest, but he saw nothing. Finally when they stopped to camp for the night, hoisting their canoes up over a downed tree for shelter, did the Frenchman confront Etchemin. He pulled the Algonquin aside and whispered to him.

"I can see you are uneasy. What disturbs you, my old friend?"

"I feel the presence of evil all around us," answered Etchemin. "It appears on one side of the river, and then I catch glimpses of a shadow, a danger. I would not be upset if we could leave the evil far behind. But it follows us down river."

"I don't understand. What are you saying?"

"We are being hunted."

***

At Etchemin's request, they stayed close to the little campfire that night. It was partly due to his superstition, and partly to the necessity of keeping as dry as possible under their canoe shelter. Jacques didn't feel the others necessarily needed to know about their guide's fears, especially since it may prove to be nothing. Jacques had known Etchemin for the better part of a year now, and had grown to trust him. But he was white, while Etchemin was native. The Frenchman didn't share all of the understandings or beliefs of the native people. Jacques had often listened to the native stories around campfires, but he had never seen anything to convince him that the spirits of the dead, be they humans, animals, or gods, would be interacting with the real world. Etchemin might be worried, but Jacques would need some proof.

The heavy rain let up after nightfall, but the cold wind continued to blow through the valley, chilling the men to the bone. Their supply of firewood had dwindled from trying to feed the fire to dry out themselves and their gear. Obviously they'd need to traverse the woods to gather more. Francois started out into the darkness collecting downed logs, and without noticing, had wandered quite a way from the little campsite. He made a few trips, each a little farther away. On his last trip, he was surprised by the sound of an animal rummaging through the underbrush a few yards away. He pulled out his little single-shot pistol, thinking about how some fresh-cooked meat would raise the spirits of their group, and tip-toed through the quiet woods in his moccasins.

A tricky characteristic of Michigan weather is how fast it can change. Storms emerge from nowhere, and in a moment they clear up. That happened suddenly, as the clouds parted for an instant, letting the light of the nearly full moonshine down on the land. Francois had a great view of the creature he was trailing. It had crawled down a little hollow at the base of an uprooted tree trunk. Not far away now, it became an easy target. He raised the pistol and took aim.

Only, he never fired. His pistol arm slowly lowered. A pair of slanted, glowing yellow eyes stared back at him from the cavity under the tree roots. Francois was stopped, staring into those eyes. They were mesmerizing—until the low growl issued from the burrow. The Frenchman had never heard anything like it. He was gripped in fear as the creature emerged, crawling out on all fours, and then standing up on its back legs. It easily towered over Francois and opened its fangs in a savage manner. He could smell its putrid breath wafting over the few feet of space between them. Francois's instincts kicked in, and he raised his pistol and fired point-blank into the creature's chest. The puff of smoke clouded his view of the shot, but when it cleared, real fear washed over him as the creature, uninjured in the least, crouched and prepared to spring at him.

Back at the fire the three remaining men jumped up at the report of the pistol. They ran into the woods when they heard Francois's screams. Etchemin grabbed a log from the fire to use as a makeshift torch so they could see their way through the dark underbrush. The scream died in the night. They arrived at the scene but could find nothing: no body, no blood, no clues as to Francois's location. The three looked all over for an hour but there was nothing to be found. Wearily, they returned to camp to sleep and search again in the light. They kept one man up on watch, rotating every few hours.

Jacques took the first watch, since there was no way he could sleep now. He kept hearing Francois's horrific screams echo through his mind. Obviously something awful had happened to his companion, but there was no clue as to what. Trappers had occasionally told stories about those who had gone mad from too many years in the wilderness. And of course some people were taken each year by wild animals, a great predator like a bear or cougar. But there should have been some evidence if an attack had occurred. None of this made sense. Finally, Etchemin relieved him and he slipped into a troubled sleep, dreaming of an elusive shadow in the darkness.

It was raining hard again, large drops pounding the surface of the river when daylight broke over the valley. The three traders searched for hours in vain, and finally had to pack up for home knowing they simply must outrun the worsening weather. Their hearts were heavy at the abandonment of their missing companion, but they could not wait a moment longer. Etchemin, who had the best skill on the water, rode alone to both steer and paddle from the back of his canoe, while Jacques and Pierre teamed up in the second canoe.

The day passed without incident, the river widening as they neared its union with the great lake. The incessant rain continued, wind driving it against them again and again. They stopped for the night only a mile from the shore of Michigana, and they could hear the huge waves crashing upon the shore even from this distance. There would be no fire this evening, as the rain absolutely poured down upon them. They tipped up the canoes again, giving them only a bit of shelter but no relief from the piercing cold. The three slept close together for warmth.

In the middle of the night, a deep, throaty howl instantly woke the three. The rain had stopped and the moonlight shone down weakly through the cloud cover. It was just enough to display the world in a vague, dim, dream-like state. They crawled out from under the canoes and there they saw it, a huge, shadowy creature stalking them from the edge of the deep woods. Its eyes glowed in the darkness, and its jaws were opened, revealing large fangs. It walked upon its two hind legs like a man, but there was nothing human about it.

Before the Frenchmen knew it, Etchemin had reared back and thrown his large hunting knife with deadly accuracy. The creature howled in pain, and staggered backward a few steps as the knife buried itself up to the hilt in its chest. Then the creature reached up and pulled the weapon out with its claw-like hands, dropping it to the ground.

That same moment Etchemin's hatchet became embedded into the creature's shoulder. It howled again as the momentum knocked it backward to the ground. The native knew there was no time to lose.

"Back to the river," commanded Etchemin. "Now!"

The three flipped and pushed the canoes down the bank and jumped in. The river might give them the only protection they could get. With all their strength they paddled downstream to the safety of the great lake, in the near total darkness. Their only hope was to get as far away from the thing as possible.

They tried to move to the middle of the rushing river, already a good 20 feet from the shore, but it wasn't enough. In a maelstrom of fury, the brush of the river bank exploded, leaves and branches flying in all directions, and the shadow creature burst forth, soaring through the cold autumn night. Its roar resounded across the water as it slammed into the center of the canoe with the two Frenchmen. Neither had time to react as the canoe flipped and splintered in half under the weight and power of the attacker. Already the precious furs and equipment were sinking and disappearing down the river. Etchemin, who had been following his companions, propelled himself forward where Jacques could grab hold of the front of the canoe and pull himself in.

Pierre had somehow reached the far bank and run shrieking off into the forest. Though they called out and paddled for the far bank, Jacques and Etchemin would never see him again. An eruption in the river pushed their canoe right up out of the water. Both men sprawled out in the air as they hit the shallow water at the edge of the bank. Jacques staggered up the bank and looked back to see his native friend suspended in the air, his limp body held up by the beast in the dim light of the moon. The creature tossed the dead body back in the river and howled again. Jacques knew there was no escape. He stood his ground, awaiting his fate, as the creature advanced on him.

***

Six months later, a thin, specter of a man staggered into

the fort at Mackinac. Surprisingly, and against all odds, Pierre had made it back alive. No one recognized the gaunt visage or the emaciated frame, rugged from living in the wild for such a long time. He was filthy and his clothes were in tatters. His skin was leathery and wrinkled. Though still a young man, he seemed to have aged decades since he last left the fort. His hair and beard were grayish-white, long and tangled, and he had a wild, yet weary look in his eyes. But his mind was affected the most. He could barely speak, and amid the inane prattle and nonsense he did sputter were lamentations for his dead friends and rantings about some deadly, wild creature.

His necklace held only half of the pointed jewels it once had when it was pulled from the earth. Pierre had traded them away, one after another, to the various tribes he encountered on his journey back north, in exchange for food and shelter. He'd had no other way to survive, since winter foraging was nearly impossible in the Michigana wilderness. His precious treasure, plucked from the burial mounds, was spent keeping himself alive.

A couple more claw-shaped jewels were traded in for a plot of land and a small log cabin inside the fort, where Pierre spent the rest of his days. It took the better part of two years before he regained his senses, and he eventually married, though he never returned to Quebec. Those few remaining relics from the earthen mound far to the south were passed down to his children, and on down the line of descent. His detailed account of the journey, including the encounters with the creature, was carefully scripted into a small, leather-bound journal. Along with the last of the jewels, the journal was mislaid amid his few belongings, and lost to antiquity.

Even though he would never see the beast again, his

nightmares would haunt him for the rest of his days. Always, he would see the initial attack on the burial mound, and he would have other dreams, fancying himself a beast of the wild running through the wilderness. And the cursed jewels, long after leaving the French traders' hands, would still call to their original owner years later. The creature would ceaselessly hunt for them until they were all returned and woe to any who stood in its way.

CHAPTER 2

January 2007

The new year started out with unseasonably warm record temperatures and no snow in the little town of Twin Lakes. Across the nation folks enjoyed working outdoors for an extra month. Carpenters were able to squeeze out a few more weeks of work, and the college bowl games were nearly all played in warm weather, regardless of the city in which they were held. On the other hand, towns in northern Michigan and other states that relied on winter sports activities to bring in the much needed tourist money were taking a beating. There was no snow for the snowmobile trails, no ice for the rinks, and the ski hills were running at a bare minimum with man-made snow, a poor substitute for the real thing, melting nearly as quickly as it could be fabricated.

Not that it didn't get cold at night. Temperatures did drop well below freezing, especially on the many clear, cloudless nights that wouldn't bring the snow so badly needed to kickstart the floundering economy again. There was no precipitation, and the bright sun warmed up everything all day long.

Twin Lakes was aptly named for the two large inland lakes that bordered the eastern and western ends of town. Carson Lake and Long Lake, connected by a short, winding river, were part of northern Michigan's inland waterway, eventually leading out to Lake Huron at the port city of Cheboygan. The two lakes, Michigan's third and fourth largest, and connecting river systems were surrounded by cabins, cottages, vacation homes, and multi-million-dollar residences. The town, relatively small in population, bloomed in the warm months as the thousands of tourists and summer residents flocked to the northern haven. Very few of the local population could afford to live on or near the water, not when property values were well over $1000 per foot of frontage.

Though the tip of northern Michigan had been settled since the 1600s, originally the edge of civilization didn't extend far from the fort and village at Mackinac. Eventually settlers moved farther inland, and as governments began to claim the developed land, surveyors began the tedious job of mapping out the inland sections. The small village of Twin Lakes was thus established as a trading site between the pair of lakes on the inland waterway. It grew slowly because it was simply a stop on the way to someplace else. But after many years, folks began to realize the value of waterfront property, be it a river or a lake. At that point, the land became much more precious, and the entire area turned into a vacation destination.

The lower peninsula of the state is unique in that its shape resembles a gigantic hand or mitten, and this has been a means of common unification among its residents. Michigan's citizens have for many years used their hand as a ready reference map to point out features, especially to those from out of state. People living on the tip of the mitt have been an independent and self-reliant folk since the area was first settled. Most are very simple, country people who just want to make their living in the world. Many moved up north to live on their own or to carve out their own space in one of the few wild areas left in the world. Others wanted to escape the overly bureaucratic nonsense and rat race of the cities. And there were always some who simply wanted to disappear.

***

Old Bill Sawyer lived with his son Mick in a run-down shack of a house on the edge of the state forest east of town. Old Bill, now in his late seventies, was a recluse who never came into town, even to see a doctor when he was ill. He relied on his 51-year-old son Mick to provide all of the comforts of life an Alzheimer's patient could get.

There were times when Mick would leave his father for days at a time and escape to gamble at the local casino. Basically he'd put out some bread, butter, a pack of bologna, and a case of Old Milwaukee Light, and his father would be in hog heaven during his waking hours. Mostly the old man slept peacefully in his decrepit, brown leather recliner, staring at the small brick fireplace and the little side window looking out into the endless woods of the backyard. But when he was awake, you never knew how long before all hell broke loose.

His body was actually in pretty good shape for his age, but his mind's elevator didn't quite go to all the top floors. On good days he stared off into the distance and maybe drooled a bit. On bad days, he ranted and raved, swearing at his son and even throwing things that were handy: magazines, coins, anything else he could get his wrinkled old hands on. Although he might forget who his son was, and he often forgot who he was, at least he could still remember to feed himself and keep the fire burning. Mick usually left a pretty good supply of split logs next to the flat, stone hearth, but Old Bill was nimble enough to go outside, traverse the three steps to the ground, and get more from the pile next to the little garden shed if necessary.

That was why Mick always bought beer in cans: he hated cleaning up the glass afterward, and he'd lose his bottle deposit. In this economy, every dime counted.

Mick took care of his father because he didn't have the cash to put him in a home. And really, there were no homes anywhere around. This certainly wasn't the big city where old folks' homes were a dime a dozen. Plus, the old man received his Social Security check each month, just like clockwork, which Mick cashed and drank away at the bar over the next four Saturday nights. Mick drove a big, orange county plow truck during the winter, and a faded yellow county road grader in the warm months. With the current temperatures being warm, he was out of work and waiting for snow. His father used to say that idle hands were the devil's workshop, and that couldn't have been more true for Mick. When he wasn't working, the flashy lights of the local casino called to him. All too often, when he had the cash, he answered the call.

And so it was a bright Saturday afternoon turned to a Saturday evening, Mick was out the door for some excitement. He left the food and beer on the small, square kitchen table. His father was asleep in the recliner, the house was very warm, and it was time to get away for a bit. Mick hadn't thought about bringing in more wood, and besides, he probably wouldn't be gone long, since he didn't have much cash to work with this time around. Mick fired up his rusty pickup and headed off toward town to fill up on gas and then head for Petoskey and the casino. Forty-five minutes later, as he pulled into the casino parking lot, the first few flakes of January's first snow began drifting down under the overhead lights. Mick's spirits rose even higher. Finally, there'd be work! Walking a bit taller than he had in weeks, he strutted into the casino for what he determined was some well-deserved fun.

***

The snow storm blew across the tip of Michigan's Lower Peninsula, covering the land in a thick blanket of white powder. Storms are often especially sudden and severe in the vicinity of the Great Lakes. Storm systems often pick up great amounts of moisture as they pass over Lake Superior and Lake Michigan and when the huge air masses are too full, they dump their precipitous load on whatever land mass happens to be under them. This accounts for enormous amounts of lake-effect snow through many of the counties adjacent to the Great Lakes. Lake-effect snow bands can even stretch far inland, all the way across the state, depending on the accompanying winds.

There was already an inch of snow on the ground when Old Bill awoke from his nap with a chill in his bones. The fire was burning down, but he needed a bit of fuel for his stomach first. He waddled into the kitchen wearing his old chinos and slippers and slapped together a bologna sandwich. He grabbed two beers and carried it all back to his recliner. Plates were beyond him on most days, especially if Mick wasn't there to force him to use one. He rested the sandwich on the arm of the chair, popped the beer tab and took a long pull. Then he pushed the beer can to its resting place between his legs and tore into his dinner. He was just finishing up the sandwich and had opened his second beer of the night when he heard the wolf howl in the yard. It was a long, drawn-out, resonant wail that penetrated the outer walls. It didn't come from far off in the woods, it was right outside. He dropped the beer can on the floor, where it spilled and puddled around his feet. He'd lived here all his life, and he hadn't heard a wolf since a trip he took out west back when he was young and spry, nearly 50 years ago. That sound wasn't right. He knew there shouldn't be any wolves around, not anywhere near Twin Lakes.

The howl came again just outside the house, and his heart began racing. The thin, under-insulated walls enabled him to hear the creature making that noise circle the backside of the house. Bill's clouded mind went a thousand ways and then blanked as he stopped and stared at the fireplace. The fire was nearly out and there was no wood inside the house to burn. Already the little house was cooling off, leaking its life-sustaining heat into the raging storm outside. How could he go outside and get more wood with a wolf running around the yard? But Bill couldn't focus on the temperature because the howl again reverberated through the little house.

And then, just as suddenly as it all started, the noise stopped. Old Bill stood in the doorway between his kitchen and living room, waiting, listening. Minutes ticked by on the little old mariner's clock in the corner, but there was nothing. No sound, no movement. The little adrenaline his old body produced eventually ran out and he staggered over to his recliner and fell backward into it, exhausted. A scare like that would nearly do him in. He shook his head a little, closed his eyes, and tried to rest for a minute.

A strange thought ran through his head. Maybe he'd dreamed it all. Bill knew he was getting old, and sometimes he didn't remember things really well. Many times he was confused about things when he shouldn't have been. Sometimes he even imagined things that Mick later told him weren't there. But there were times when he knew he was okay and his head was clear. He felt that clarity now, but maybe this whole event was just a part of his imagination. He raised his hands and lightly rubbed his eyes.

Just when he thought everything might just be okay, he heard a scratching at the windowsill of the little window next to his fireplace. He'd lived here for most of his life, and he knew his house intimately, regardless of the comings and goings of his mind. He knew that sill was about six feet off the ground. There's nothing that could be scratching at that window that wasn't very, very tall. When he dropped his hands and opened his eyes, he looked right at the face of death. There in the window was a creature he'd never seen in his life. It seemed like a great dog or wolf, and yet its visage seemed almost human too. Hauntingly glowing yellow eyes blazed at him from the middle of the dark, furry head. It seemed to have a snout, though not nearly as long as that of a wolf. Black hairs sprouted crazily from its cheeks, its muzzle, and its head. The creature's paws were on the sill, the claws sunk deeply into the soft wood. It appeared to be standing there, not simply hanging from the window. Bill's eyes opened wide as the creature opened its jaws and let out another bloodcurdling roar.

Bill's mind didn't blank out this time because the intense pain in his chest kept him sober. He realized he was dying right there, and yet he couldn't move. His eyes were locked on the glowing orbs of the creature. His last thought was that the creature appeared to turn up the corners of its mouth in an awful grin, a far too human-like grin.

When Mick finally returned home many hours later and found the body, fear wasn't even considered as a cause of death.

Inside the casino, with no windows to the stormy outside world, Mick had found a streak of luck at blackjack. He'd continued the ride all night and well into the next day, finally losing nearly everything just as hunger hit him. He took his few remaining dollars over to the buffet and there realized how long he'd been in the casino. He ate quickly and departed for home. The snow storm had settled down into a light flurry of flakes, and the emergency road crews had plowed out the major roadways. Tired, full, and yet glad that he'd be back to work in the evening, Mick sped back to check on the old man.

***

Joe Thompson, the chief of police, along with one of his deputies, and the county coroner met Mick at the house about a half-hour after he returned home. Mick was beside himself over his father's death, but the chief couldn't find any wrongful death. Yes, it was quite irresponsible of Mick to leave his father alone like that, but it wasn't criminal. Mick would have to live with that guilt the rest of his life, and the chief thought that was probably worse than any punishment the law could impose.

They found the body right where Old Bill had dropped dead, in his recliner. His eyes were frozen wide open, as was his mouth. His body was stiff in rigor mortis, and very cold from the refrigerator-like interior of the house. His lips and fingers were blue.

Mick had cleaned up the spilled beer out of habit. He hadn't thought it might be any sort of evidence the police might need to see; he just knew he had to clean up another of his father's messes, though this time he was dead.

The county EMS ambulance drivers zipped up the thick black body bag, lifted it into the back, and closed the double doors. Mick stood on the small front porch and watched them pull away, followed by the police cruiser. He continued to stare out at the yard and woods for a long time, lost in thoughts of his father, until the cold of the evening reminded him he was wearing only a t-shirt. He was about to head inside when he looked down around the small shrubs at the foundation of the house. He couldn't for the life of him figure out why there were dog tracks all around the little house. They didn't own a dog, and there wasn't a neighbor with a dog for miles around. He wouldn't notice the deep scratches on the window trim for another few weeks.

The coroner's report officially labeled the cause of death as accidental—hypothermia. There was no investigation and no autopsy. No one would know Old Bill's heart stopped. No one would know what he saw that actually scared him to death. In this part of the world, accidents like freezing to death did happen to the old and infirm every winter. They were tragic, true, but in northern Michigan amid simple people with simple lives, such incidents were bound to happen.

***

The remainder of the month of January certainly made up for its quiet start. The snow continued to build up steadily, and frigid temperatures and the subsequent wind chills kept many in the warmth of their homes. The snowmobile riders and skiers from downstate and out of state returned in vengeance, trying to make up for lost time. Finally, the local residents who badly needed the winter tourism money could get their businesses back on track.

Old Bill Sawyer's tiny obituary was buried in the back of the local paper. Being a recluse, his name was noticed by only a few locals, mostly neighbors who knew him.

Not making the paper was the report of a local farmer's livestock killed by what appeared to be a rampaging coyote. On the last day of January, temperatures dropped to -12 in the Twin Lakes area, and wind chills forced them well below -30. Tom Watkins Sr., owner of a 40-acre farm just a few miles away from Old Bill's home, awoke early in the morning to begin his daily routine of chores. After a steaming cup of coffee, he bundled up and strode out to the barn to feed the animals and collect eggs. When he saw the sliding door of his barn opened, he immediately cursed his son Tom Jr., whose job it was to feed the animals at night and close up the barn, for his laziness. Several chickens lay slaughtered in a bloody mess on the floor, and there were claw marks in the wood planking and on the edges of the poultry cages. On the bloody goo of the barn floor and in snow all around were the tracks of what Tom believed was a large dog. Since there were no wolves in the area, it had to be a coyote, though they were generally scavengers, preferring something else to leave them a meal. But with the frigid temperatures, a scavenger couldn't pass up an easy snack even if it had to kill it itself. With the barn door left open, it was an open invitation to the buffet.

Tom Jr. maintained he had indeed closed up the door, as he did every night. He still pleaded his innocence when Tom Sr. slapped his bottom several times as a reminder of how important it was to pay attention to details.

Yes, the Twin Lakes area was a simple area, with simple folks. They believed in what their eyes told them, they believed in good hard discipline, and they believed they lived in a safe corner of the world.

**

Steve Nolan needed a break from grading semester exams. Next semester, he'd definitely write them up in an easy-to-grade multiple-choice format. That was a common mistake for a first-year teacher. But he learned fast. His juniors and seniors' end-of-the-year tests would certainly not take up this much time from him in June. He picked himself up off the comfortable recliner and stretched, popping several joints in the process. After several hours of grading papers and sitting in one position, he stiffly made his way to the fridge for a cold soda.

Though he grew up in the Upper Peninsula, Steve's family had great ties to the tip of the northern peninsula. His grandfather's family had lived in Mackinac City and Carp Lake for many generations, back to when the area was first settled. His wasn't a large family, nor did many stray from northern Emmet and Cheboygan counties. When the job opened at Twin Lakes High School, he immediately applied for it.

He even carried a special heirloom of his family, worn on a chain around his neck. It was a deep black gem, speckled with red veins. It didn't look very valuable, it certainly wasn't priceless or flawless by any means, but it was passed down the generations, an old antique and relic of the frontier days when explorers picked their way through the primeval forests of what is now the upper Midwest and Great Lakes region. It may not have been worth much, but it always was a conversation piece, especially on dates. Women could appreciate a man with ties to his family and past.

Steve had lived in Michigan all his life, and even though he did travel and vacation all over the country (and the islands of the Caribbean), there was just no place like his home state. Sure, mountains, oceans, and hot sandy beaches were great, and he always enjoyed getting out of Dodge, especially during the cold winters, but there was nothing like Michigan. Perhaps it was the swift changes in the weather, or the grand change of seasons, or the outdoorsman's playground of lakes, rivers and natural wildlife. Maybe it was the down-home folks, or the sound Midwestern values. Maybe it was the novelty of having your state map attached to the end of your arm. Nothing anyplace compared itself to Michigan.

He was just returning to the mundane chore of grading

the advanced science papers when a pair of headlights turned down his little driveway and shone through the large bay window of his apartment. Finally they're here, he thought. I have a real excuse to take a break! Steve still had all the next day to finish up the papers before grades were due on Monday. He slipped on his boots and heavy winter jacket, leaving the tedious work for later, and strolled out into the cold to welcome his parents.

His parents had made the long drive from the little town of Stambaugh, far in the western end of the UP, to celebrate his twenty-fourth birthday. They didn't travel often, and their only son saw them only on holidays and family occasions. But when they did get together, it was usually a grand affair. As was the family custom, the birthday boy chose the restaurant, this time a Chinese sit-down in the nearby city of Petoskey.

They rode together in his parents' old station wagon. Though Steve was only about six feet tall, he towered over his mother, and was of course offered the front seat when they traveled together. That was great, because the back seat usually smelled stale and musty, like an old sweaty sock was hidden under the cushions somewhere. And the way back of the station wagon, well, it was better not to mention it at all. Sometimes Steve was amazed that the family truckster could still make the trip. Despite the rough exterior, and the often stinky interior, the wagon's engine had the heart of a lion, and after 16 years, it still kept plugging along.

Steve's father, Tom, had many hobbies, everything from making sausage to amateur astronomy to refinishing his 1960 Chevrolet (its various parts had kept a place of honor in the pole barn since 1988). But mostly, he just enjoyed brewing his own homemade beer and, of course, consuming it while sitting on the front porch and watching the sun set. Tom was always coming up with new ideas for quitting his job at the post office, making money, and becoming his own boss. At one point, he was going to open a small diner specializing in late-night breakfasts. But their little town barely supported one small family restaurant, so that idea fizzled. Another grand idea was to quit and start up a Christmas tree farm. Nope. He'd even tried to get a cell phone tower built on their property so they could collect rent. But that, like everything else, didn't go anywhere. So Tom continued to work at the post office, smiling and being friendly with everyone who stopped in, but secretly wishing he was someplace else.

Steve's mother, Alice, was a year away from retiring from teaching third grade. She'd been in the same school for most of her career, and had gotten to the point where the children of the kids she once taught were now in her class. That was enough of an incentive to retire.

Steve and his parents ordered their drinks and favorite Chinese dishes when Alice, always an avid reader, skimmed over the placemats with their descriptions of the Chinese zodiac and yearly astrological signs.

"Oh, I just love these Chinese calendars," Alice cried. "They're so interesting! They change so often, and you know their predictions are almost scary they're so right on." She looked carefully at the dates emblazoned on the circular yin/yang pattern that resembled a clock with animals where each numeral should have been. She was a bit disappointed. "Let's see, Steve, you have the sign of the pig for your birthday this year!"

Steve rolled his eyes. Wonderful. He could be a pig all year.

His dad, who carried far too much useless information in his head, saw Alice's mistake right away. "The change of the Chinese year doesn't occur until February 18th in 2007. Right now it's still 2006, according to this calendar. That puts Steve back one animal character."

Where his dad came up with these things Steve would never know. Hard to believe a postal worker's brain could store such a vast array of utterly pointless trivia. Maybe it would serve him well if he was ever on a television game show. "So what sign do I have to look forward to on this birthday?" Steve asked innocently.

Alice seemed quite pleased he wasn't the pig anymore. After a few moments of reading over the calendar, she beamed. "Why, honey, for you it's the year of the dog."

CHAPTER 3

February 2007

Most people who have spent time on or around the interstate know about the large elk herd that populates the high hills between the little villages of Wolverine and Twin Lakes. The huge, majestic animals can stand up to five feet at the shoulder, and weigh up to 800 pounds, making them quite an obstacle when they decide to cross the highway. The animals are rarely in a hurry, preferring to graze along the hills and lick the road salt built up along the roadside. Drivers heading north on I-75 especially will often see several of these great animals at dusk, just as the last few minutes of daylight are falling behind the hills on the west side of the highway.

But of course, the animals don't just live along the freeway. They meander through the woods and small open spaces, mostly to Bruder Road, which runs parallel to and between 50 and a hundred yards from I-75. Though there are few residents along this unpaved gravel road, plenty of wildlife, including the majestic elk, are more frequently seen there than on the busy freeway.

A dark Thursday evening found Clayton McGowan speeding north on Bruder Road, heading toward the overpass and town. His little mid-sized pickup was traveling a little faster than conditions would normally allow, bouncing and slipping along the hard packed snow covering the gravel. The many back roads of the county were highly crowned, making it easy to drain the rainwater from them in the spring, summer, and fall. But in the winter, the same crown often caused many vehicles, and most every school bus, to slide off into the snow banks that rose up to four or five feet above the road's surface because of the snow plows. Snow days were more commonly due to the slippery back roads than to the heavy snow fall.

Clayton had just taken his eyes off the road and was just adjusting the radio to another country station when the elk stepped out into the narrow road. It was indeed a huge beast, its head and neck easily taller than the cab of the little pickup. If it saw the truck bearing down on it, it gave no indication. The elk just kept slowly crossing the icy road without a care in the world. McGowan looked up in time to see the rear end of the huge animal, easily the size of a large horse. He slammed on the brakes and swung the steering wheel to the left, knuckles turning white from the death grip on the wheel. Luckily he missed the hind quarter of the animal by a few inches, which saved his little pickup thousands of dollars in damage. But unfortunately for Clayton, his vehicle jumped right up onto the bank at the side of the road and embedded itself nose first several feet into the snow.

The elk sauntered its way across the rest of the road, stepped gracefully up the bank, and disappeared into the woods to the east, apparently oblivious to the chaos it had just caused. Just before it departed, it turned its head back once and snorted, warm breath puffing a cloud from its nostrils. It obviously didn't think much of Clayton or his truck.

Clayton took a minute to clear his head, blinking his eyes and wriggling his jaw. He mentally checked himself out, then unclicked his seatbelt and tried to push his way out the driver's door. However, it wouldn't budge. The door, as well as the entire front end, was buried in snow up past the top of the wheel wells. He'd have to wait until spring to get out that way. So Clayton crawled across the little bench seat and tried the passenger side door, which opened right up. It didn't take long for him to appraise the situation. He was stuck good, and it would be a long, cold walk into town if no traffic came his way. Grabbing a flashlight out of the glove box, he slid out of the pickup and down to the hard, packed road. He took a look around him to see if the elk was still around, but it had left quite some time ago. Clayton buttoned up his thick, brown barn coat and began the long walk to town, praying somebody would drive his way.

About five minutes later he first heard the footsteps crunching in the snow off to his right side. It was faint at first, and he thought he was hearing things, or that the crash had scrambled either his brains or something in his ears. He stopped, shook his head, then rubbed his ears one after another with the palm of his hand. Nothing. Must be my ears or my imagination, he thought as he started up again. But within a few steps he heard it once more. There was something following him, slightly crunching down into the snow. He looked around and shone his flashlight in the direction of the sound, but saw nothing. Clayton made up his mind that maybe he should pick up his pace, and he hurried down the road. However, the faster he went, the louder and closer the snow steps became.

On a whim, he stopped and swung his light back to the snow bank at his right rear. There he finally saw two bright lights shining back at him in the darkness. But they weren't quite lights. As he squinted, attempting to see further, the little lights blinked. They were eyes!

Suddenly, more brightness reflected back to him from beneath the eyes. Whatever it was had opened its mouth, revealing long, yellowish-white fangs that shone in his flashlight's glare. A low growl emitted from between the teeth. Clayton instinctively began backing away from the creature, until the back of his knees came in contact with the snow bank and he fell backwards onto his rump. The flashlight dropped from his cold hands and he lost sight of the creature. He knew it was still there, and that he was in a compromising situation.

Clayton scrambled to his feet, still backing up in the snow bank, but now his feet were sinking in, up past his boots. The growl from across the road repeated, only much louder this time. Clayton snapped as fear gripped his mind. Forgetting everything else, he took off, sprinting through the deep snow into the woods toward the interstate. Even though his breaths were labored and loud, and adrenaline was flooding his system, and his boots smashing through the crusty snow reverberated through his head, he could hear the creature jump down onto the icy road and follow him into the woods. He ran with all he had, leaping through the two feet of thick whiteness, arms and legs flailing as he tried to clear the encompassing snow.

***

The sales rep was heading north on I-75 to Sault Ste. Marie. The driver had left Toledo, Ohio, several hours earlier, and was looking forward to a good night's rest before his meeting the next morning. The major drug company he worked for paid him well, but they also gave him a huge sales area with many, many miles to traverse each month. After a long day in the office, the 300 miles of driving had been causing him to yawn for an hour now. He had the radio turned up loudly, and even opened his window every few minutes to blow fresh cold air across his face. He knew he didn't have far to go. He could make it to the next exit in a few miles and pick up a new coffee to replace the last one he'd gotten in West Branch.

The night was pitch dark, the sliver of a moon completely hidden behind dense storm clouds. The headlights of the little sedan provided the only illumination for miles around.

His car roared along the freeway, heading to the top of a large hill, and the driver was just rolling up the window when something dark and brown lunged out into the road from behind a road sign on the right side of the highway. He was upon it with no time to react. His sedan slammed into the body, flipping it over the dash and up over roof. Senses returning, he hit the brakes, sliding into a spin that left his vehicle turned around facing south. There in the headlights was the crumpled shape of what looked like a man lying on the road.

He slowly got out of his car and walked over to the body. Then he turned his head to the side and threw up. He had hit a man, and the bloody remains were there on the road for all to see. He fought to keep his head from swooning, then pulled out his cell phone and called 9-1-1.

***

The chief of police was out of bed and on the scene within 20 minutes. Joe Thompson had held the position for 14 years now, most of which had been quietly leading to his retirement. Sure, the Twin Lakes area was a hotbed of activity during the summer months, and all of the craziness was hard to keep up with. But for most of the year, he kept a quiet watch over his sleepy little town. He liked it that way. Not much trouble to deal with, few major incidents to handle. He was not one to be easily trifled with, and no one, either local or tourist, messed with him. His intimidating six-foot four frame easily carried 280 pounds. He was truly a massive man. Though he was graying around the edges, the hard lines of his face hid all emotion while he was working. Mostly now he looked tired, but that was only the mask that everyone saw. Beneath the surface, he was always ready for action.

Chief Thompson lit another cigarette, its tip glowing against the blackness of the night. He'd vowed to quit as his New Year's resolution, but it didn't take long to backslide. His top deputy, Gary Meade, had already secured the scene, and another patrol officer was backtracking the dead man's footprints through the woods and back to Bruder Road. The Medical Examiner had arrived, declared a time of death, and was otherwise occupied with the grisly details. A tow truck was hooking up the sedan for transport back to the police station.

The mangled body was identified from the driver's license in the man's wallet: Clayton McGowan of Wolverine. A little later his flashlight and pickup were found back in the snow bank on Bruder Road.

"I never saw him coming. He was just there. There was no way I could stop," the driver repeated over and over. He was obviously in shock. Killing a man was not a part of his plan for the trip up north. Chief Thompson actually felt sorry for him. Yes, he was a tired driver, but McGowan had emerged from the woods in a shielded spot behind a road sign. His brown jacket had hidden him until the last moment. And judging from the distance between the footsteps, the man had been running top speed toward an appointment with death.

But evidence would be needed to be picked over carefully. Though the chief didn't believe there was a crime here, he still had to process the scene because it was the prosecutor's office that would determine if charges would be filed. The chief's opinion didn't matter much compared to that of the prosecutor's office up in Cheboygan.

The chief shook his massive head as the sales rep was driven off to the police station. His sedan was towed behind, and the ambulance drivers cleaned up the human mess on the freeway. Accidents could always happen; they had happened a lot in his 28 years of service. But this one was more than odd. Why on earth would McGowan or anybody for that matter, be out tramping around in the woods and run out onto the freeway? It was at least 50 yards of deep snow and a five-foot wire fence to cross over to get to this point from Bruder Road. It didn't make any sense. There was always the possibility of drugs or mental instability. An autopsy would hopefully provide some answers.

At least, it didn't make sense to the officers at the time. It would still be a few months before more pieces fell into place. The tracks the deputy found in the woods alongside McGowan's certainly didn't seem out of place here. Everybody knew the woods was teeming with wildlife, especially elk and deer near the highway. Besides, the punched-through holes in the snow wouldn't reveal what type of animal had passed that way. They certainly didn't resemble a dog's tracks, but then again, no one expected to find a large dog's tracks in the vicinity anyway.

The creature was not a wild dog, nor a wolf or coyote, and truly not a werewolf, at least not in terms that Hollywood always set on such creatures of myth. Its emergence had nothing to do with the full moon. Like any other nocturnal predator, it hid during the day and was active at night. It did not fear crucifixes, garlic, wolfs bane, or any other of the infamous remedies made famous in the movies. It could not be killed by silver bullets, or regular bullets for that matter. It was a supernatural combination of an otherworldly specter and a wild, ravenous creature. Though it had the appearance of a gigantic, wild canine, it had many human-like characteristics too. Its paws were more like hands, and it could stand up on its hind legs. And probably the worst of all, its muzzle had the unnatural ability to make many of the same facial expressions as humans could make.

***

The next two weeks saw a flurry of snow and ice storms. They battered the tip of northern Michigan with a fury, causing several snow days for the kids and a large number of messy vehicular accidents. Even some businesses closed down, as no one was out shopping anyway. Though wreaking havoc, the storms left behind a beautiful façade on the landscape. The glistening ice buildup on the tree branches pulled them right down to the snow-packed ground. Then on top was the thick, heavy snow that gave everything a puffy, contoured profile. Many of the narrow back roads appeared to be tunnels carved from ice as the trees leaned down over and crossed to the other side.

Though the harsh weather would keep many inside, especially the locals, it attracted a different kind of audience.

A dim, ghostly light began to grow through the tree line until it bathed the woods in an eerie, translucent phosphorescence. Suddenly the frigid winter night air and the calm, silent forest were split with a high pitched scream, the whine of a snowmobile engine. The whine grew in intensity as not one, but eight snow machines darted down the snow-packed trail. The recent snowfall provided a few inches of excellent powder for the sleds to glide through, spraying the fine white particles for yards around. Of course, the downstate folk couldn't resist heading up north for a weekend in the perfect weather for hitting the trails.

The lead snow machine swung into a wide spot of the trail, and the rider waved on his companions. It was the universal signal that a momentary pit stop was in order, and everyone else who could hold it should keep going. The other seven riders waved as they passed, and though they didn't stop, they did slow a bit so the front rider would easily catch up a few minutes later.

He killed the engine, swung his leg over the heavily padded seat and stepped to the edge of the trail where the tree line began. It took nearly 30 seconds to unbuckle, unzip, and push aside the various layers of warm clothing before exposing his groin to the frigid air. After bouncing and skipping over bumps, dips, and even small logs for the past three hours, his bladder was more than ready to be emptied.

Steam from the warm liquid hitting the snow bank rose quickly up into the air as he rolled his head back and around in a circle, his stiff neck giving out little pops. Talk about relief! His whole body seemed to sigh and relax as he finished and began the chore of bundling back up.

He'd finally zipped his outer layer, a brand new jet black snowmobile suit trimmed in green, when he heard something moving in the woods off to his left. He paused, listening intently. Spotting and watching the wildlife was always one of the great thrills of being in the north woods, and most snowmobilers relish the opportunity to see local animals, since most are hidden, scared off by the noisy machines. But unlike most other riders, he was a city boy, and his attraction to snowmobiling was the adrenaline rush of speeding over frozen ground. He really could care less about critters, and like many who grew up in the "civilization" of the city, deep down he feared the wilderness and the various wild animals, especially anything bigger than a raccoon. However, this wasn't something raccoon-sized or smaller. That primeval fear now came thundering back into his mind as he realized the heavy, crunching snow steps had to belong to a large animal or even a person. Out of hope for the latter he spoke out to the woods, "Is somebody out there?" His voice came out far more timidly than he had anticipated.

He could now hear the breathing, a deep, heavy exhaling, almost like a blast of wind against a windowpane in the winter. Every few seconds the breathing was mingled with a low, raspy growl. The noise continued to move slowly through the woods, circling around the clearing, always just behind the line of fir trees.

Slowly, he backed up to his snowmobile, and carefully straddled the big machine while still looking into the woods. Just after securing his helmet, he noticed a pair of lights shining back at him from the tree line. He couldn't help but be pulled in by the little, yellow beams gleaming at him out of the darkness. They had a luminescence all their own—there was no light shining on them to reflect. All other thoughts were stripped from his mind. He forgot his companions; forgot the crunch of an animal's footprints. He was totally captivated for what seemed minutes, until the lights blinked. That brought him back to reality. Those were eyes staring at him! He freaked. He was here in the deserted, frozen north to race his sled, not be dinner for some animal. He fired up the snowmobile, which immediately leapt forward and bounded off down the trail.

It was not a moment too soon, because the tree line exploded in a tempest of snow and branches whipping and swirling in the light breeze. The eye of the storm was a dark, shaggy form that crashed into the snow bank on the opposite side of the trail, where the snow machine was parked only seconds before. The creature righted itself, shaking off the powdery snow, and tore off after the machine. It was streamlined, head leaning forward and down to knife through the wind. The powerful legs galloped rhythmically, propelling it through the wooded trail. Seeing the creature run, no one could imagine those muscular legs, so adept at striding on all fours, would enable it to stand erect and upright.

On an impulse, the rider looked back over his shoulder and nearly fell off his vehicle in shock when he saw the lights of the creature's eyes following him down the trail. Luckily his hands were tightened in a death grip on the handlebars. He whipped his body back around and gunned the engine. He'd kicked it in while flying across wide open fields, but he'd never had his sled cranked up that fast while on twisting, turning trails.

He glanced over his shoulder again very quickly, and was horrified to see the eyes still behind him. They were about twice as far back as before, but it didn't register with the rider. They were still following him, even though he had his sled nearly topped out. Speed was his only option to escape. He pushed his snowmobile beyond the limits of safety. No one in their right mind would ever tear off through a dark forest, unless his life depended on it. He didn't look back again, but concentrated instead on traversing and negotiating the curves and bends in the trail.

Minutes dragged on as he sped ahead, frantically searching the darkness ahead for the tail lights of his companions. Panic overwhelmed him. Though he was flying through the trails, time seemed to have stopped to a crawl. His only thought was escape. He prayed. He promised he'd change his life. He'd do anything to make it back home alive. He just hoped to never see those bright golden eyes, or the creature they belonged to, ever again.

Just when he thought he'd totally lost his party, his machine rounded a bend and the lights of the gas stations and fast food restaurants of Twin Lakes flashed out of the darkness. He kept the snowmobile gunned until he reached the Twin Lakes Trading Post, slowing down as he recognized the others in his party. He whipped around the group, only stopping when they were between him and the dangerous forest.

***

He slowly raised his head and looked up the hill at the full moon rising over the tree tops. His sinewy neck muscles easily raised the heavy furred head. As he viewed the intruder digging furiously into the soil, he could feel the hatred welling up inside his being, like steam rising over a pot of boiling water. "Trespasser," his mind screamed at the man. But all that came out through the long jaws was a deep growl that made the man look up, startled. Easily seen through the bright moonlight, the man's eyes widened in fear, and he stumbled backward, falling to the soft, wet grass of the hill.

Steve advanced up the slippery slope of the hill, surefooted and confident. This intruder had trespassed and now must be punished. Trespasser. Again, the deep growl emitted from his throat, and the man seemed to be fumbling in the deep hole he had dug, unable to escape, his frontiersman's trousers caught on something. Steve had almost reached the summit of the mound and was looking down on the man.

Somehow the man, the trespasser, freed himself and turned to run away, to escape to the safety of the river beyond. Steve grinned, knowing the man could never escape. He crouched, his powerful legs leaping over the pit, then springing for another leap that would pin his prey. As his arms reached outward and up, claws spread wide, the man tripped and rolled, looking up. Steve, a furious and dark creature now, grinned again at the helpless man as he prepared to meet his fate.

Steve Nolan bolted upright in bed, his body sweaty and breathing heavily. His eyes were wide open, though he wasn't looking at anything in particular. The dream again. The same dream he'd had as a young teenager. Always the same. He hadn't had that particular nightmare in years, 10 years in fact. Even though he'd had that dream more and more frequently during his fourteenth year, he'd since forgotten about it. Or, better yet, forced it out of his mind. As a youngster, he'd been almost afraid to sleep at night, fearing he'd have that awful dream again. Of course he couldn't tell his parents about the dreams. They'd probably make him to go therapy or something. He didn't want to join that particular group of kids. It was easier to just deal with the nightmares himself.

Always in his dreams he was running through and among the trees of a dark forest. In his subconscious state, he knew it was the deepest darkness of night, yet he could see in a ghostly, surreal way. One set of dreams was always like this, like watching the black-and-white negative of a movie strip. And though the scenery of his dreams changed, it was always the natural world: running through the underbrush, ducking low through fields, feeling at one with nature.

The second type of dream was in vivid color and full of sounds. The last rays of the setting sun cast deep reds and violets across the sky and lengthened the shadows of the forest. Or the first bright golden rays of the morning fingered through the branches. He was searching for something, always looking. He checked every settlement, every inhabitation, every person for the missing thing. He was never sure what it was he was searching for, just that it was very important.

The last dream was always the same. This one was by far the worst, and he would have it more and more frequently as the year wore on. It was always night in this dream. He could hear the gurgling of a small river or stream. The full moon shone down upon him so he could see clearly up at the man digging into the top of the dark, grassy hill. In this dream, he crouched to attack this oblivious person who was dressed in some old fashioned frontiersman's garb. The man was trespassing, disturbing the spirits (how he knew this he'd never understood), and the man had to be stopped. A low growl would echo through his mind, and when he saw the man look up at him, his frightened countenance would be lit up in the moonlight.

When he was 14, the dreams were awful, but he attributed them to his love of vampire, werewolf, and monster movies he stayed up late watching on weekends. Years later, Steve looked back and figured they were much more a product of teenage hormones. His parents never knew about the dreams. An adolescent boy, he kept them to himself as he kept everything to himself. Besides, his parents wouldn't understand.

It was because he never brought up those dreams that Steve never found out about the dreams he had when he was four years old. These were totally removed from his mind, hidden in the deepest, darkest recesses of his subconscious. It was a horrible time for him and his parents alike. Had he asked, his parents would have reluctantly shared this dark period with him, and of course would have suggested having him talk to someone about the recurring dreams. But he didn't ask, and so he never knew.

Please, Lord, Steve prayed, his hands slowly washing down his face from his forehead to his chin, don't let these dreams start up again.

CHAPTER 4

March 2007

The first weekend in March was a blessing for the people of Twin Lakes.

Ted "Sonny" Chambers was finally found after being missing for two days. Luckily for the 48-year-old Sonny, he was spotted early on the morning of March 3rd before he completely iced over by a lone ice fisherman slowly wandering the shoreline of the frozen lake. Sonny was easy to distinguish even from a distance because of his long gray beard, which reached halfway down his chest, and a nearly bald head with only a few wisps of white hair randomly poking out in all directions. This appearance always added about 20 years to his real age. He wore a thick, green flannel over shirt, traditional gray long johns for pants, and thick wool socks inside his boots, but no coat, no hat and no gloves. Obviously he wasn't dressed for a cold night in Michigan winter.

Of course, Chambers' disappearance was all over the news. Folks had been combing the deserted woods and frozen marshlands around his home all during the slowly lengthening daylight hours. After a few days, most had given up on him, figuring his decaying body would show up after the spring thaw. But, the human spirit is resilient, and sometimes the body will kick out enough natural chemicals to keep the muscles going long after they should have stopped. Adrenaline had propelled

Sonny to travel over 12 miles through thick, heavy snow drifts to reach Long Lake from his little cabin at the edge of the state forest. Deputy Gary Meade, second in command at the little police post, had the fortune of following the old man's tracks, at least as far as they lasted through the blowing and drifting snow. Indeed, Chambers, it appeared, had walked (or run in some places) that entire distance.

As it was, Sonny had frostbite on both feet, his fingers, and on his ears. He was on the edge of hypothermia, having been outside in the snow for nearly 50 hours. He was in a state of shock, most notably from exposure to the cold, but he had also developed a twitch that his friends had never noticed before. His hair was up on end, while his eyes were wild and flitting, constantly on the move, from left to right, and he began looking far off into the distance, as if searching for something that was just out of eyesight. He even raised himself on tiptoes to look over the shoulders of those around him every few minutes. He had never been one to converse much, and many people who knew him (or knew of him) had hardly ever heard him say anything at all. So it was no surprise that he had clammed up even more after his exposure to the elements.

He was taken by ambulance to the local hospital in Cheboygan for emergency care. Though he did end up losing two toes to the frostbite, Chambers recovered, at least physically, after a few weeks. However, if the doctors had been able to probe into the deep recesses of his troubled mind, they'd have seen the reason he'd never speak more than a smattering of gibberish again.

Sonny had been hunted.

He had been out working in his wood-heated garage, which was hotter than Hades the night he left. The one-stall garage was too small for his pickup, so he had totally enclosed and insulated it a few years ago and basically added on a work room to his cabin. He lived alone, and so he often worked in his hobby shop in not much more than his underwear. He enjoyed carving wooden sculptures and making birch bark lamps that he'd sell at the local craft fairs around the north during the summer.

Severely injured in an auto factory mishap in Lansing several years ago, Sonny was retired and collecting Social Security and long-term workman's comp. His back and rib cage had been crushed in the accident, and he couldn't lift 50 pounds if his life depended on it, even after months in a hospital and years of physical therapy. Though quiet and introspective to begin with, Sonny's injury kept him speechless for many months, a habit that carried over to his new lifestyle where he rarely spoke to anyone. The former football player at Olivet College aged nearly overnight into the shell of an old man, and of course his beard made him look even older. His financial settlement did allow him to move north to Twin Lakes, where crafting and fishing were now his life's greatest pursuits. He was liked by the people who knew him, and he could be always counted on to smile and wave at anyone passing by.

Now, however, he was a different sort of recluse. He was trapped in the safety of his mind because of his encounter with the creature. Even his doctors were baffled as to the cause of his winter wandering.

On that fateful night, he'd been building a little birch lamp in the early evening when he heard the light scratching at the door. He first thought it was someone's dog, perhaps left outside and wanting to warm itself indoors while its owner was called to come over and return it home. Sonny set down his tools and sauntered over to the door, flipping on the outside flood light, but there was nothing there, only a set of dog tracks all over the snowy step. A light fluttering of fluffy, white precipitation was falling, and it was slated to get much worse over the next few days.

Sonny always had a soft spot in his heart for little animals, and so he called out for what he was sure was a lost dog, alone in the storm. When no answer came, he slipped his stocking feet into his heavy swampers and walked around the side of the garage, following the tracks. Still nothing there. He was ready to head back inside when he first heard the snarl. It echoed through the wooded yard and driveway for several seconds, and was the most vicious, horrible sound Sonny had ever heard. It sort of gurgled as if there was too much saliva in the way of the growl getting out. And it came from above him.

Looking up to the roof of the single-storied ranch house, Sonny saw the glowing yellow eyes of the specter of death glaring down at him from above the door to his workshop. It was too dark up there, and of course the floodlight in his eyes prevented him from seeing the entirety of the beast. But Sonny knew enough to know he had to flee right then and there. There was no getting back into the safety of the house the way he'd come out.

Boots unlaced, still in his long johns and luckily wearing a flannel top, Sonny bolted off into the woods away from the creature. He ran as fast as his legs could take him, high-stepping through the snow drifts. Unluckily for him, his sprint took him further away from civilization and from any homes where he could find sanctuary. He was headed into the forest.

After a few minutes, he stopped to catch his breath and rest. And then he heard the footsteps crunching in the snow behind him. Again, he took off, running into tree branches and larger limbs that nearly knocked the wind from him. He went as far as he thought he could, then stopped again, only to be herded again a few minutes later by another crunch of steps through the crusty snow.

Most of the night continued in this fashion. The snow continued to fall. When daylight finally broke over the horizon, Sonny could see he was deeply lost in the state forest. Everything looked familiar and yet unfamiliar at the same time. His mind was in a fragile state already, but the frigid temperatures and wet, sloppy precipitation pushed him over the edge. He continued his wandering, moving more in a circle than actually getting anywhere. Finally, out of exhaustion, he plopped down under the boughs of a huge pine tree, crawled into a ball and fell asleep.

It was nearing darkness again when he awoke, cold but somewhat rested. Sonny was roused from his hiding place by a haunting growl, quite too similar to the one he'd heard only 24 hours ago. It was too near for him to just stay put. He had to flee again. But another night of restless running through the woods had completely done him in. Every sound was the creature, every broken branch was it stalking him, every whine of wind through the trees was its breath, hot on his trail.

Finally, the next morning, an old ice fisherman saved his life, though Chambers' mind, reeling from the sight of the monster, wouldn't return to rational thinking for a long time. Luckily his body, conditioned from the years of sports and rehabilitation, refused to quit. Despite his former injury, the adrenaline had kept him going. Almost mindlessly, his body kept on pushing through the deep snow, fear driving him through the windy night.

As Chief Thompson read through the deputy's report, he couldn't help a strange feeling in his gut. This was the second wanderer in almost as many weeks. His mind flew back to Clayton McGowan. Was there some sort of connection here?

Both men out for a nice walk in the country, except neither one had any reason to be outside in the freezing temperatures in the first place. Okay, so McGowan's car broke down, but why run through several feet of snow and over a wire fence to the freeway? And what reason could Chambers have had for being half naked?

It didn't make sense.

But at least this strange incident had a good ending, or at least not a horrible one.

***

Three weeks later, another encounter would not end so happily.

Chet Parker crouched low through the underbrush. His boots crunched lightly on the little snow that covered the ground. Even though the March temperatures had warmed, it was still cold enough each night to freeze. Light gusts of tiny snowflakes often swirled in the late winter breezes, sometimes blowing up from the ground and at other times floating down from the branches or the clouds overhead.

Poaching was nothing new to Chet. His rusting house trailer sat in a clearing at the end of a two-track at the end of a dirt road. It was surrounded by various piles of junk, including a beaten-up old washing machine and every redneck's welcoming signpost, a '78 Chevy sedan up on blocks. His family had owned their property outright for several decades, and it passed down from generation to generation. He was the last surviving member of the family after his mother passed 10 years earlier. That made the property his outright. The 48 acres technically made Chet quite a rich man. He could have sold part or all of it and made a small fortune in the past; land prices in northern Michigan were certainly at an all-time high, and vacant land was being snapped up by the greedy investors and downstate people every day. Now, however, his unpaid back taxes, compounded over several years, made it difficult, if not impossible, for him to make any sort of gain. That, and he had no desire to move. He liked his solitude. This was his home, had been all his life.

The bright red droplets of blood absolutely screamed out against the brilliant snow. Twilight has that effect on ground snow; it nearly glows and sets off anything around it. The slowly rising near-full moon gave an ethereal feel to the world. Tracking in the last of the day's light, especially through snow, was a simple chore. It was just a matter of time before Chet found the doe. If anything, he was patient.

The fact that his property butted up to thousands of acres of state land with few roads or trails made poaching that much easier. Venison and game birds, and even the occasional varmint, allowed his meager wages to keep him living in the trailer. It wasn't just that he didn't have much money to work with. Chet was fond of the local cuisine. He preferred the sweet taste of venison to beef any day. It was ingrained in him from his youth, when his father and he shared time in hunting camp, which was really just a shack a mile out their back door. They'd fry up venison chops and steaks in butter with onions and peppers grown in their little garden behind the rusting trailer. The memories made Chet smile warmly, a contrast to the cool, crisp air.

His shot wasn't the greatest; it was a bit hurried, in fact. Something had spooked the doe. Chet refused to believe it was him, even though he'd had a weird sensation just before pulling the trigger of his rifle. A little shiver had run down from the nape of his neck to the small of his back. This was easily explained, and attributed to the cold, and the fact that he dressed more for the anticipation of spring than the wrapping up of winter. But nonetheless, he had hit the doe with a killing shot. It had staggered, almost falling, and then found a surge of adrenaline while bounding its best away through the woods. The cold (and the shivering) quickly forgotten, Chet began trailing what he hoped would be his suppers for the next few weeks. He had all the skills and gear necessary to gut, clean, and prep the deer, and his freezer would be filled up again soon. The blood trail on the brilliant snow was an easy track. Reminding himself how his stomach would growl in the near future if he messed up, he forced himself to patiently follow the trail.

He had shot the doe just three hundred yards from his home. It was a short walk to his bait pile. Now in his later years, he didn't feel nostalgic enough to use the hunting camp his father had built. That was just a part of what sometimes seemed ancient history. Besides, it was too long of a walk. He poached for food, and though he didn't worry too much about being caught by the law, the closer the kill, the shorter distance he had to get it back unnoticed. Generally, no one came within miles of his land, but the times, they are a-changing. People nowadays wandered all over the countryside and stuck their noses into all sorts of things that didn't concern them. You never knew if or when you'd suddenly come across a hiker, day fisherman, or, God forbid, another hunter using the state land, oblivious to Chet's private hideaway. He didn't want to take the chance of spending time in jail (and the court costs) he didn't have.

The reeling doe wasn't going far, and its escaping life blood would only allow the hunter to find it that much easier. Chet followed the trail down a bit of a gully and into a swampy area. He knew the land like the back of his hand, and he was nearing the state property. That was no big deal; you could legally hunt there and track down a kill. However, that was during hunting season in November, and certainly not in the middle of March. The swampy land was mostly frozen underfoot, so Chet couldn't sink too far into the mud that did accumulate in the warmer daylight. He continued on for another 10 minutes, ducking under branches and around the dense thickets he couldn't push his way through.

Light gray clouds had covered the sun all day, and now as they parted the moon shone through, illuminating the land. Darkness and shadows began to blur at the distant limits of Chet's vision. He could see very well up to a few dozen yards, but beyond that the thick trees added to the darkness. Another hundred steps and his doe, lying prostrate on the ground, began to come into focus. Chet ducked under a large branch and then he saw it clearly. It had fallen with its back to him, half-hidden at the base of a large fir tree. About 10 yards away, he stopped abruptly. Something wasn't quite right. The deer hadn't simply run out of energy and dropped over. It had fallen where he had stopped, right here, and then had been dragged the last 30 feet to the fir. Chet cocked his head a bit to the side in bewilderment. What the hell? He could see the blood trail stop at his feet and the snow crumpled up where it collapsed. But then a definite bloody sliding track, like a sled zig-zagging behind a young child, led to the doe. He studied the situation for a few moments, completely stumped.

However, his pondering was suddenly interrupted by a low rumble. Chet's first thought was that it was far-off thunder, but when he looked up and saw the moon he shook his head. Not quite, not a storm in the area. The sound had come from the direction of his doe. He heard it again, and this time his mind registered it as a growl. A low, guttural growl. It wasn't very loud, but certainly enough for him to hear clearly at this distance. It continued for a few seconds. Again, he cocked his head to the side as the hair on the back of his neck stood straight up. What the hell indeed?

The darkness continued to descend on the woods, but Chet hardly noticed. His attention was fully focused on the point ahead of him where his kill rested beneath the great fir tree. As he looked more closely, he noticed the carcass was slightly shaking from side to side. Then a violent tug shook it, and its head flapped down and away from him. Chet took a cautious step forward, and this time the throaty, unearthly growl resonated loudly through the woods. It was a sound unlike any he'd ever heard in his life. He knew all about the various predators in the north woods. He and his father had hunted bear, and they'd killed plenty of coyotes and bobcats in years past. He'd never heard a wolf up close—there were only a few in the lower peninsula, and those were far to the east, over by Lake Huron. Besides, they howled. People in newspapers had sworn they'd seen cougars before, but that was another unproven myth in this area. This, however, didn't sound like anything those animals might create. It was barely an animal sound. It was deep, and it chilled him down to his core. It came again louder, more menacing, and then the deep green bows of the fir began to part, and Chet absolutely froze in his tracks.

A dark, hairy shape, slowly and yet easily, forced itself up over the carcass and through the branches. It was a darkness, so pitch black that it stood out even against the shadows of the dark tree. And yet, the face of the creature was lit by piercing, glowing yellow eyes focused intently on him. The eyes were large, but slanted, slightly squinted as if sizing Chet up. The darkness of the face parted and the creature's jaws opened. It was then Chet understood. The blood dripping from its maw and staining its fangs dripped down to the doe. It had captured Chet's kill, dragged it under cover, and claimed it as its own. And Chet had interrupted its feasting. It had just torn out a chunk of flesh and devoured it. It gave out another growl, and Chet could swear it actually curled up its lips and gave him an evil smile. Even at this distance he could smell the rotten rank of its breath. He felt the warmth of fear flood over his body.

He had forgotten about his rifle even though he held it in a death grip in his right hand. How many seconds he stared into those eyes he could not tell. A sudden coldness over his crotch and legs broke the spell. He had wet himself and hadn't noticed until this moment. The creature raised its head a bit higher, and Chet saw its paw reach forward and cover the doe's shoulder. Paw wasn't the right word, though. It was huge, much larger than that of a human. And it had fingers, for God's sake! Covered in the same dark fur, each was several inches long, and ended with a curved, bloodstained, black claw. There was even an opposable thumb matching the digits. The paw (hand) curled, the claws easily piercing the doe's hide, and pulled the carcass a few more inches toward the tree's base. It was protecting its kill and warning the human to get away, fast.

Chet didn't need to think twice. He may have forgotten about his rifle right there in his hands, but his instincts didn't fail him. He slowly backed up, feet retracing his own steps as the creature glared at him. He hoped against hope that it would stay right there and enjoy its dinner, and leave him the hell alone. He suddenly thought about the nice, comfortable lazy-boy in front of the wood stove in his trailer. Just get me out of here, he thought. Though he didn't know it, his body took on the gestures of supplication. His left hand was up, palm outward to show he was no threat. He was in grave danger and even as a hunter he was clearly out of his element here. God help me, he thought over and over. His head bowed slightly, as did his back and legs. He made no quick or sudden movements. He wanted to show he was not here for a confrontation. He even tried to walk without making any sound, though the crunching of the snow at each step made him wince. He kept his eyes locked with those of the creature. Wrong place, wrong time, that's all. Just let me slip away, God, please let me just slip away, he thought.

Chet backed away slowly, continuing past the point where he could just barely see the glow of those monstrous eyes. Another step and they were gone. He forced himself to backtrack another 20 yards, in what seemed like hours, far enough to make a run for it, when he stopped abruptly. He had backed into a tree. Trying his best to maintain eye contact, his peripheral vision told him he couldn't have hit a tree. He was stepping basically in his own footprints. He looked down to make sure. His left hand slowly and naturally reached behind him, but it wasn't the rough bark of a tree his fingers encountered. He felt rough, long, coarse hair. Chet's eyes closed, as his entire face attempted to squint and his shoulders shrugged over and downward. The rifle dropped from his hand as the reek of rotten flesh wafted over him from above. He didn't need to hear the low guttural, now too-familiar growl to know his time was up.

***

He glanced from beneath the tree boughs at the new intruder snaking his way through the snow. Moonlight glinted off of the barrel of the rifle held cautiously in the intruder's hands as he crouched and peered into the darkness of the hiding place. Through the gnawing hunger Steve's mind blasted out a warning, "Be gone," but all he heard was the deep guttural growl. He tore off another piece of flesh, trying desperately to satisfy the appetite that gripped him. He must feed constantly to maintain the high level of energy expended in the cold winter.

Despite the warning, the man crept closer, interrupting the feast. Steve's mind, losing control from the insatiable need for sustenance, gave out. He rose up on his haunches and pushed aside the tree boughs. This was his kill, and he'd defend it to the death. The woods reverberated with the last human thought before losing the battle with the subconscious beast. The deer had already been dead when he found it, but now the need to kill overwhelmed all rational thought.

The intruder began backing away, but he was now the prey. Steve crept out of his makeshift den and circled wide around the prey. The scent of his urine, his fear, dissipated through the woods, making him an easy target even in the darkness. A few silent bounding strides brought him behind the prey. Another second and the intruder would be in his grasp.

Steve awoke breathless and sweating yet again, his hands gripping the bed sheets. He stared wild-eyed at the ceiling, trying to regain his thoughts and composure. The first of the day's light was filtering through the curtains, illuminating the room with a ghostly aura. He could never remember his horrible nightmare of the hill evolving into a nightlong saga involving another person, another time and another place.

The reality of the dreams was the amazement and the horror. They were so lifelike, with every sense stimulated, that it was as if he was actually there and was reliving the memory. He could never understand his own role in the dreams, how or why he was such an aggressor. Nor could he understand the beastly nature of his surreal dream existence.

Steve was the only person to ever see Chet Parker again, and it was only in his worst nightmares. No one filed a missing person report. No one even wandered onto his property for over a year, and even then the overgrown lot was given up to abandonment. With the back taxes piling up, the acreage was eventually auctioned off at the county courthouse. Chet had disappeared without a trace.

CHAPTER 5

April 2007

As the calendar flipped from March to April, the Michigan weather roared in the new month with a late-season snow storm. Nearly a foot of new snow fell upon the bare, muddy ground that had at last shed its previous white skin. It was too bad, because all of the school kids had finally released their pent-up energy from cabin fever during a two-week warm spell. Now they were back inside the stuffy classrooms watching thick, slushy snow cover up the first sprigs of green grass.

Steve Nolan took the wintry opportunity to strap on his old-fashioned, wooden snowshoes and get in one last day of plodding through the back trails. Through the winter, he would snowshoe through the various mile- and two-mile-long loops in the woods south of town or at the local county park. But this particular Saturday, he had an itch to thump around for a bit longer. The two-week warming spell had re-energized him, and the latest storm wouldn't dampen his spirits. He threw a small lunch and a few bottles of water into his little day pack, formerly used in his collegiate days. Then he drove out east of town to the edge of the Crooked Creek State Forest. He'd yet to try the trails out here, at least in the winter, but heard they were excellent. He heard there were trails for miles that would lead all the way to Gaylord if you were really ambitious. It was almost as if he was being called out there, summoned to this particular woods. For the last hike of the winter, he wanted a special trip, one he could remember until the snow returned next November or December. He'd certainly get all of that and more.

He parked his little red truck at a small turnout, strapped on his snowshoes, donned his heavy winter jacket and pack, and set out down the bright, snowy path. His dashboard clock had said one thirty when he exited the car, and he'd had to wear his sunglasses to block the extreme glare of the sun as it hit the wet snow. The slush made it hard going, and it didn't take long before he was working up a sweat that cooled his skin as it evaporated.

Steve plowed his way through the narrow trail for nearly an hour before stopping for a needed break. He made short work of one bottle of water, guzzling it down in just a few big gulps. He was just unwrapping a chewy granola bar when he quivered, not in a cold way, for he was more than bundled up for the weather, but because something was irritating him, itching in a way that caused him to crane his neck out and upward.

For some reason, the skin just below his neck was stinging, so Steve paused to check it out. He unzipped his heavy jacket and pulled down his collar to see his necklace, his family heirloom, which rested on the irritated spot. He reached in to scratch his chest, and lightly touched the gemstone. It was surprisingly warm! Granted, he was working out pretty hard here, but the stone itself was emanating heat, and that was causing him to itch. Well, he couldn't have that, so he reached around his neck and unclasped the leather thong, bringing up the little stone to eye level. He cocked his head to one side in curiosity. The normally black gemstone was glowing with a faint yellowish light. The red veins seemed to pulse with an unnatural beat, like some tiny, misshapen heart. And it continued to emanate a diffused heat, as if it had sat out under a hot sun all day. Steve stared at it, drawn into the luminescence of the object as time seemed to transcend around him. He was lost in the beauty of the golden, alien light.

That was when he noticed the sky had clouded over. A cold breeze began to whistle through the thin, bare trees. Something didn't quite feel right. He shook his head to clear himself from the enchantment of the stone and perceived that he'd been here, rooted in this spot, for quite some time. He pushed up the thick sleeve of his jacket and his eyes widened when he noted it was now 6:30, according to his wristwatch. How had four hours slipped by him without notice? He shivered again, but this time it was from the frigid air that tingled the exposed skin. It was getting dark. He immediately bundled back up, slipped his necklace into a pocket, and spun around to return quickly to his truck. He didn't have any sort of light out here, and he'd need to make good time back if he didn't want to get lost in the dark.

He high-stepped his way in return, and luckily the matted prints of his snowshoes enabled him to dash back to his vehicle. Though he made good time, the thick and dark cloud cover hid the daylight much earlier than normal. Dusk was falling rapidly around him, and the forest took on a peculiar, sinister visage. The trees, still weeks away from budding, reached out their bare branches like thin, boney, and grotesque arms and fingers. Of course, they were animated into life by the wind which was picking up.

Finally Steve spotted his truck about a hundred yards down the trail, the bright red paint sticking boldly out from the monochrome environment of white and black. That was when the low howl rolled across the little valley, echoing off the large oaks and maples. Steve stopped, listening intently. It lasted for a few seconds, but thankfully, it seemed to be coming from a distance away. That didn't stop him from hustling on his way, however. With darkness looming, Steve didn't want to encounter some wild animal out here in the middle of nowhere.

He closed the distance halfway when the howl came on again; this time it was much louder, much closer and much more defined. Steve could hear a guttural rasping to the creature's cry. Whatever it was, it was following him, and he had no intention of meeting it. His brisk jog turned into a flat out run, hampered as he was by the large, paddle-shaped snowshoes attached to his boots.

The red truck, now a distinct symbol of safety, drew nearer as he ran. Twenty yards. Ten yards. He broke out of the trail and fell over onto the hard packed snow of the road, fumbling with the straps around his boots. The safety of the truck was suspended because he'd never get in the cab with the snowshoes still on his feet. A third time, the creature's wail pierced the cold air, and this time it was a loud, long growl that sent shivers up Steve's back. He had to get out of there, and fast!

At last the snowshoes peeled off his boots and Steve jumped into the cab of his pickup. He fired up the engine and floored the gas. The little pickup jumped to life, spinning a donut on the slippery two-track and then fishtailing back to the main highway. Steve's heart was pumping from the tension and the panic, and he was sweating from the exertion of his run from danger. He never looked back, and shot out on to the highway without stopping. He'd have been ticketed for sure if an officer had been around, but luck was on his side again this night. As he reached the lights of town, he finally regained his composure.

The following morning, the sun rose full and warm, any traces of the dark cloud cover blown far off to the east. As quickly as it had come, the snow melted and spring returned. The school kids were able to start having track meets and ball games. Steve Nolan slept deeply after his strange encounter in the State Forest, and after a few days of his memory becoming obscured by getting back to his busy school routines, he had to wonder if it was all just a dream anyway.

***

Katie Brandon's son Isaac meant the entire world to her. She was a single mom, and Isaac's father disappeared soon after the announcement that she was pregnant. She'd raised the boy all by herself for seven years, and with a little help from her parents, she provided a meager life for them both by waitressing in town. Luckily for her, a kind old neighbor three houses down was more than willing to watch Isaac while she worked. Mrs. Anthony was in her sixties, having raised her own five children as well as several of her grandchildren. She loved kids, and couldn't help being a grandmother to her neighbors' kids too. She had no need for money, telling Katie on several occasions to save more to provide for her son.

They lived in a little subdivision, a curved lane that connected with the highway at both ends. All of the houses on the highway side had big fences to keep the kids away from the passing traffic that flew by at all hours. All of the houses on the woods side had big backyards that opened to the thousands of acres of state forest land. Mrs. Anthony's house had a big fence, and Katie's backed up to the woods.

Katie's one day off was Thursday, as she tried all she could to pick up any extra hours she could get. Those few days off she spent entirely with her son. Even when she had mundane chores to do, they always were right next to each other. This day, she was paying bills at the small, round kitchen table. Isaac had his crayons and paper out and was practicing being an artist. In between writing checks and stuffing envelopes, she asked him, "What are you coloring there, sweetie?"

"It's the wolf man who lives out behind the shed. I see him out the windows at night sometimes."

"And what does he do out there?" Katie asked in that absent way moms do when their mind is on something else entirely.

"Sometimes he walks around. Sometimes he hides behind trees. And sometimes he runs around like a doggie."

That caught her attention. She turned to look over at his drawing. Something about the picture didn't look quite right to her. The thing on his paper was dark brown and black, obviously furry from Isaac's shading (he always paid attention to detail), and it had tall, pointy ears like a dog's. But what really drew her in was its eyes.

"Are his eyes really that yellow?" she asked him.

"Yup, they even glow when it's real dark out." He continued to color in his masterpiece, shading the grass a dark green.

"He seems awfully tall to be a wolf man." She tried to laugh it off a bit, but it didn't sound quite right, to her anyway. "How do you know he's that tall?"

"'Cause sometimes he comes right up to the house and looks in the window." He pointed at the dining room window. "He smiles at me too." Isaac pulled up the corner of his mouth in a horrible grimace, showing off his teeth.

Katie was instantly horrified. Her eyes got real big real fast, and her heart started racing. This wasn't right at all. Isaac was not one to tell stories, and he always told the truth, even if it got him in trouble sometimes. She looked out the dining room window, which was a good five feet above the ground, and past the little patio with her lounge chair, past the toys in the yard, past the storage shed, and into the woods beyond. Even though the day light was bright, the woods seemed a little darker today, a bit sinister even. No, this was definitely not right. She just had this feeling that something really bad was out there to have given her son such an image to draw.

Katie kept her son inside the rest of the spring, much to his dismay, and drove to the neighbors to drop him off or pick him up, rather than walk the three houses over. She went out that weekend and bought new thick curtains, and drew them well before dark. Luckily, and for the first time since Isaac was born, they went to her parents' house downstate to spend the summer.

***

The warm days and cool nights of April always brought out the Tucker clan's spring male bonding ritual, 'coon hunting. It was a time-honored tradition shared by the men of the family for many generations. Since most of the family lived within 10 square miles of each other, it was easy for the Tucker boys to grab a few six-packs, load up the shotguns, and take the beagles and blue-ticks out into the woods that surrounded their homestead. Raccoons were abundant on the family's property, just bordering the edge of the Crooked Creek State Forest. There were so many of the annoying critters, in fact, that many made a nuisance of themselves by becoming road kill.

Basically, the dogs did most of the work, trailing and tracking the fat, masked critters until they tried to escape up a tree. Once treed, the dogs would bay at its base until the good old boys arrived and did in the raccoon with a well-placed shot from a .22 or a .410 rifle. Not that it was exactly sporting, but it did allow the many brothers and cousins to get together, pound back far too many beers, and shoot something. It was big-time entertainment for this time of year. Deer season was just too long a wait for them.

Technically the raccoon season is from October 1st to January 31st in Michigan. But an addendum to the law states that private property owners can hunt or trap the animals without a license or permit any time on their property if the critters are doing damage or about to do damage. Of course, the Tucker family was well aware of the technicalities of the law. Every raccoon they killed was obviously considered to be "about to commit damage."

Old Marv, the balding patriarch of the family, generally didn't take part in the hunt anymore, but he did keep a large urn of strong, black coffee, a cooler filled with ice and beer, and a big pot of hot, spicy chili stewing out in the decaying gray barn out back of his property. His sons and grandsons would be needing a thick, hearty snack when they returned from the cold woods, triumphant with their quarry. He listened to the oldies on the little radio in the windowsill while his beefy arms kept a slow, rhythmical stir around the chili pot. Yup, family was important to the old man. He was so glad to be surrounded by the men he was honored to call his boys. They meant the world to him.

This third weekend in April was to be young Cole Tucker's first 'coon hunt. He had mixed feelings on the matter. On one hand, he was excited to join his dad, his older brother Alex and all of his uncles on the trip. It meant that after 12 years, he was finally becoming a man. They'd look at him and treat him differently after this, just as they did with Alex a few years earlier. But Cole was also apprehensive. He'd never killed any creature before, nothing besides little bugs and spiders anyway, and he knew from three years of Alex's hunting stories that he'd have the honor of shooting down the first 'coon of the night. Whereas Alex had no problem hunting and killing, Cole wasn't sure he relished the thought. And afterward, he'd have to learn to skin it. Yuk! But the need to be accepted by the men of the family eventually wore him down. He could do it, he thought. He'd have to do it.

Just after darkness fell, the large group of men and boys piled into several pickups, baying dogs in cages in the back of each truck. Several of the uncles and cousins had already begun the night's festivities with a bit of liquid refreshment, and a few would undoubtedly be half in the bag before the first 'coon was treed. Cole couldn't help but be enraptured by the excitement, bouncing along the back trails of the property, listening to his family as they chatted over their walkie-talkies.

In a few minutes, the small fleet of pickups parked in the matted grass of a trail head, and everyone disembarked. The hounds were released, tearing off into the night. The men did all they could to keep up with the dogs' baying, dissipating into the darkness, while toting along their rifles, spotlights and various refreshments.

Cole brought his own large flashlight, though his father Warren carried the rifle. Cole would undoubtedly be given his first rifle after tonight's hunt. That was the rite of passage in the family. But for now, he'd use his father's .410. They stepped carefully around logs and sharpened tree branches, avoiding the natural depressions and holes in the soil. It was amazing, Cole thought, that they could even find the dogs, being that they were so far in the lead. He strained to hear any sounds from the animals in the distance. Mostly he could hear the other men whooping and hollering through the woods. They were really living it up. Alex was already far ahead with his favorite uncle John, their light skipping over the uneven forest floor several yards farther on. The two of them were quite a pair, Alex and John, nearly inseparable, and had been for many years.

The minutes sped by as Cole and his father eventually caught up to the baying of the dogs. The hounds produced a different howl when they had a raccoon treed, letting the hunters know exactly what they'd found. Already a group of men were gathered under the boughs of a great white pine, lights trained up 50 feet or more, searching for the critter hidden in the branches. Of course they'd waited for young Cole, as this first kill would be his. Finally, the animal showed itself, and the multitude of spotlights gave it no place to hide.

Warren handed the rifle to his son, and reminded him of the proper technique for shooting. Aiming nearly straight upward was far more difficult than Cole had imagined. He had fired rifles many times in his life before, but each time was in target practice on a level plane. It took him a few extra moments to train his eye on the small, furry target splayed in the bath of light. The raccoon had nowhere to go, no place to conceal itself. The boy thought carefully about his aim before putting his index finger to the trigger. This was it, his big chance to become a man of the family. He hesitated, envisioning the first real animal he was going to kill. Suddenly, he wasn't sure he could do it. Was this truly what he wanted? Or was this for his dad, his brother, his family?

At that moment, a loud howl reverberated through the woods, more or less causing Cole to pull the trigger. It was like the cry of a wolf or coyote, only deeper, more throaty, and harsher. It was anything but far off. In fact, the howl seemed to have been created only a few dozen yards away. The distraction was plenty enough to shatter his concentration and produce a wild shot. The dogs went crazy, barking wildly as they raced off into the woods in the direction of the sound. The men had forgotten Cole's big moment, no longer caring about the fate of the 'coon. After a look around at each other, they took off after the dogs. Something bigger, and potentially more sportive, had stumbled into their laps. This was something they couldn't pass up!

Slightly disappointed, Cole handed the rifle back to his father, who patted him on the shoulder and said, "That 'coon isn't going anywhere. We'll be back in a bit, and you'll get your chance. What do you say we go see what all the excitement's all about, huh?"

Cole smiled up at his dad, mostly glad for the reprieve. He wasn't sure how to feel about it all. But he didn't have much time to ponder it right now. They stalked off together through the tall trees, following the mad rush of the other relatives who were eager to see what prize the dogs would lead them to.

The dogs were going crazy. Cole could hear them up not too far in the distance. It was funny, listening to them in the darkness. He could have sworn they sounded like they were actually fighting with some creature. They were just supposed to tree it. As they got closer, a few horrifically painful-sounding yelps were heard among the commotion. That sure didn't sound right. A few paces ahead, a set of flashlights caught their attention, and they turned to see what was happening. Two of Warren's cousins had trained their beams downward on a dark, quivering object. Cole pushed between two of the men and glared down at the bloody carcass of one of their blue-tick hounds. It had been literally ripped apart. Deep gashes covered its hide from what was left of its head down to its midsection. Its abdomen was slashed wide open, entrails and gore splattered all over the ground. Cole backed up from the shock, then turned and threw up. This certainly wasn't the way the night was supposed to go.

More loud yelps and cries from the dogs, mixed with the loud growls of the prey and the hollering of the men, continued to permeate the darkness. Flashlight beams were wildly bouncing all around the woods. To anybody watching, it would have seemed like some scene from a sci-fi movie. Obviously this battle between the animals was being waged over a long distance and time. Warren guided his younger son to follow his two cousins toward the cacophony, which seemed to be moving through the woods, from hollow to hollow. They came across two other dogs, dead, in much the same condition as the first they'd found. Whatever this creature was, it certainly could defend itself.

They stopped when the ringing of rifle shots split the air. Instinctively, Warren crouched and pulled Cole close to him. More shots rang out. A funny thing though, thought Cole, I don't hear the dogs anymore.

When they looked up, father and son could see the beams of light in the distance, only they were much more still in the darkness. The men had stopped running, and were just shining the flashlights around slowly and methodically. A minute later Warren and Cole arrived in a small glen to find a grisly scene. The family members were all there, beams of light displaying the carnage all around. The bodies and remains of a half-dozen dogs were strewn about the little clearing. The ground was soaked red with blood and hair and other unnamable limbs and body parts. Cole gagged again, turned, and threw up.

***

Several men were gathered around Uncle John and Alex, who had apparently been the first on the scene. Both still had a tight death grip on their rifles. Alex was mumbling several, seemingly incoherent things. He was obviously in shock. "It stood up and grinned at us...those eyes...shot it over and over...didn't kill it...wouldn't go down...it just took off."

Uncle John was much more lucid, and narrated the story to the others. "We got here and this *thing* was tearing the dogs apart. I put the light on the thing, and Alex just unloaded on it. I know we hit it 'cause it stumbled and fell over backwards. But then it stood back up, and I swear, it got up on its back legs. It was standing, I tell you! Its eyes were glowing, and it curled up its lips at us. I swear, I think it smiled at us. Then it shook itself and took off through the woods."

The rest of the men didn't know what to believe. The story sounded just too ridiculous, but there was evidence all around them that something had killed all of their hunting dogs. And it wasn't like John or Alex to lie, or tell stories. Plus, they were badly shaken up. Just the look of terror on their faces proved they must have seen something there.

No more was heard from the creature that night. After a few long minutes of calming down, the men gathered up the dogs' remains in the large gunny sacks originally brought to hold all the raccoons they planned to bag. They returned in quite a somber mood. The dogs weren't quite loved as pets, but they were valuable members of the hunting party, and they'd be missed terribly.

The next day, a couple of cousins retraced their steps through the forest and were able to track the creature for quite some distance by blood and paw prints. Eventually the tracks led to a small creek where the trail was lost.

Cole's big night had turned out quite differently from what was planned. There was no more 'coon hunting that spring. Though the others recovered fairly easily, Cole never took to hunting. And it was a long time, years in fact, before the boy would venture out into the woods alone. His own nightmares of scary beasts howling in the dark would haunt him for most of the spring and summer.

CHAPTER 6

May 2007

Steve Nolan's first hour astronomy class held an outing once each month to stargaze, providing there was decent weather. In fact, luckily for them all, the poor northern Michigan weather had postponed the previous four sky and star watches. The last time the class had met on Lookout Hill was at the beginning of December, and a great night that had been. The weather was perfect; a warm front had moved in and pushed off the normally cold after-Thanksgiving evenings. This allowed for higher than average temperatures, surprisingly with crystal clear skies. Stargazing was at its optimal. And to top it all off, the northern lights gave off a playful yet spectacular show for the students.

This night in mid-May was almost as spectacular. The warm, late spring breeze met the students with the promise of the coming summer months. Already, most of the trees and shrubs were blooming, a sea of endless shades of green stretching as far as the eye could see. And the sun set was truly awesome. The few low-lying clouds on the horizon looked like fiery brush strokes of red, orange, and violet. It would be an excellent night for stargazing.

Fourteen students out of the 22 in the class had shown up this evening. Attendance wasn't required, and as they met out of school, each drove his or her own vehicle; they began the show at 10 o'clock PM. It made for a late night, and a sleepy first hour the next school day, but Steve knew it was better than doing this on a weekend night. Besides, because many students would have plans that didn't include anything remotely connected to the academic world, Steve knew that the likelihood of any additional "party favors" showing up on a school night was considerably reduced. He knew his students well, liked them all a lot, and trusted them. But he also knew there were plenty of drug and booze users among them. It didn't make them bad kids. It was just sad, really, that there was so little to do in this small town that the kids turned to drugs and booze to escape the realities of their boring lives. And it wasn't a peer pressure thing either. The kids didn't need to goad each other to experiment or use; it was just accepted practice. But luckily, most students were respectful enough to the adults in the community that they'd never try to pull something like that, especially if a teacher was around.

You found Lookout Hill by driving 12 miles down County Road 53, a curved, bumpy dirt road, after heading east on the state highway 11 1/2 miles out of town. C-53 looked much like most others in the area: a few farm houses and trailers situated on and divided by large acres of scrub land. Rolling countryside made it an ideal spot for the deer to intermingle safely with the few cattle and horses safely behind twisted wire fences. Though the homes were not close by any means, they became fewer and farther between as the dirt road headed south into the thousands of acres of the Crooked Creek State Forest. About two miles from the highway a small, red, rectangular sign proclaimed the entrance to the property of the State of Michigan, along with the usual rules and regulations about motor vehicles, camping, and land use. At that point, the county road narrowed down to little more than a glorified two-track, with barely enough room for two vehicles to pass easily. The great old oaks, maples, and birches, interspersed with a few evergreens, grew right to the edge of the steep banks, two feet or more above the dusty road. Protected for decades, the hardwoods thrived, grew tall and strong, and in many cases their branches interwove themselves with the branches of their cousins across the road. Sunlight filtered down in the late fall, winter and early spring, but when the leaves opened up fully, the road, essentially a tunnel, would be dark and cool through the summer months, with the sun completely blotted out.

Though one wouldn't know it from the endless continuum of curves and chatter bumps, County Road 53 eventually connected to the state highway east of Gaylord. However, it was anything but a shortcut. Driving 30 miles an hour was sure to rattle your bones and teeth, and going more than 40 could prove fatal if your vehicle skipped, spun, and flipped. Another hazard was the hardwoods themselves; undoubtedly, there always seemed to be a gigantic oak right on the corner of each sharp curve of the road. More than one had claimed a vehicle wrapped around it, and yet the trees endured. That was the greatest testament of the state forest. The trees grew and thrived and lived through most anything man or nature could throw at them.

The rolling landscape was the same in the forest as outside it. However, about 10 miles south on the county road the hills became larger with more space between them. Then the forest opened up into several clearings. This was a favorite spot to park and watch the massive elk herds as they grazed. Dozens of the huge animals gracefully sauntered out of the woods in the early evening, and several vehicles could usually be seen on the side of the road, occupants enraptured with the antics of the wild beasts. Lookout Hill rose a hundred feet above the tallest of the surrounding hills and gave an impressive view of the entire state forest. Reached by a walking trail from the end of a small sandy parking lot, visitors parked and walked their way up to the see the most spectacular scenery for miles around.

The still blue-green waters of the Crooked Creek flooding were the only discrepancies from the endless rolling waves of the green forest. The hills and valleys gave texture to the hundreds of acres of pristine wilderness you could see with your naked eye. Even a set of binoculars wouldn't enable you to see town. The hill was a place for inspiration, often used by poets, painters, and other artists. Lovers enjoyed the quiet solitude. Someone in the past had built a wooden picnic table and a bench looking down the hill to the west. And at night, at the highest point in two counties, and miles from any town or city's light pollution, the stargazing was unmatched.

Mr. Nolan's students parked and walked up the trail to the hill, where Steve was already set up with his star charts and telescope. The sun had set behind the horizon, and the deep purple and red of the sky darkened with each passing minute. Already the brightest stars were apparent in the blackening eastern sky.

Each student group took its chart and began looking over the evening's activities. As always, Mr. Nolan began with a tale from mythology. "Tonight, since we haven't met for quite a while, I thought I'd share a scary one. I want to tell the story of the first werewolf." This brought a few snickers from the students, but at least they were all intrigued. Steve went on: "In Greek mythology, there was a king named Lycaon who ruled Arcadia, the central mountainous region of the country. Lycaon was a cannibal, who like many humans in mythology, believed himself above the gods. He and his family founded a huge cult consisting of human sacrifice and cannibalism. They ruthlessly ruled central Greece, killing off any opponents and naysayers. Zeus, the king and great judge of gods and humans, heard the cries of the victims and came down from Olympus to investigate. He found these rumors to be fact, and decided to reveal his identity to the cult.

"Most of the members immediately bowed down to Zeus, but, Lycaon was not convinced he was an actual god. Remember, he believed himself to be at or above the level of the gods. He prepared a feast for Zeus consisting of human flesh. If Zeus truly was a god, he would recognize the meal and decline to eat it, since cannibalism was one of the greatest sins men or gods could commit. Zeus immediately noticed what the feast consisted of and punished Lycaon and all his followers. They were banished to the countryside and changed into wolves.

"Just wait, it gets even better," Steve continued with a smile. "Some stories even went as far as noting they could change their form from human to wolf, depending on the time of the year or if they had eaten human flesh. Lycaon was afterward represented as an evil spirit, and his family the first to take the wolf as their sacred totem."

"Now, the constellation we focus on tonight is Lupus, the wolf. It is named for king Lycaon, whom Zeus punished in the myth. If you look to the south, just below Scorpio and Libra, you will see two dim stars. Check tonight's star charts if you're having trouble. The entire constellation is not visible, unless you're at the equator or in the southern hemisphere. But we can see a bit of it, and of course, the myth is great."

The students took turns looking through their star charts and binoculars and searching the southern sky for Lupus. One at a time, they glanced through the powerful telescope Mr. Nolan had focused on the constellation. After the featured constellation, they returned to those star groups they had previously studied. The students had fun, they asked good questions, and Steve felt pleased by the evening's activity.

***

Finally, after an hour of searching the black, starry sky, Steve called it a night. If they stayed out too much longer, he knew a number of them would sleep right through morning classes the next day. Of course he would have liked to sleep in as well, since his recurring nightmares had been constantly reducing the amount of good sleep he was lucky to get at all. The students packed up their belongings and trudged back down the steep, sandy trail to their vehicles. Steve waited until all of their cars and trucks were fired up and heading out before leaving the sandy parking lot. He was taking a different road back to town, a shortcut he'd found back in the fall. It was much bumpier, with more twists and curves, but it would arrive back near the expressway. As a bonus, he could shine a few deer in the fields with his high-powered spotlight without all of the kids scaring off the animals. There were times you could see hundreds of deer in the fields; it was just amazing. Steve would never hunt at night, and poaching was never even a thought in his mind. Some deep-down part of him just enjoyed watching the deer.

Amanda and Ben had piled into Jessie's ancient station wagon and torn off down the dirt road back toward civilization. They were the last of the students to leave. The three had been good friends since late elementary school, even though they had many different interests. Since Twin Lakes High School was small, they could each do their own thing and yet hang out as friends.

The car acted sluggish as they drove back toward civilization. For some reason, it never failed to act up when it was a long distance from home. The old wagon bounced and stuttered over the chatter bumps, those long stretches of little, rippling ridges on the dirt road caused by the melting run-off. Hard as a rock, they rattled the passengers' teeth, and certainly did not help the condition of the station wagon. The chatter bumps mercifully ended, to the passengers' relief, when suddenly, a shadow flashed across the road in front of the headlights.

"What was that?" Jess hollered from behind the steering wheel.

"What was what?" replied Ben and Amanda. She hadn't seen it, and Ben was zoning out in the back seat.

"That, right there!" The shadow flew back across the light beams. Then, to everyone's amusement, they realized they were watching an owl flying down the road in front of them. Its large brown form swooped back and forth across the road, flying about halfway down between the overlapping tree boughs and the hard pack of the road. Its great wings pumped up and down, keeping its bulk suspended. They slowed the car down to keep pace with the bird. All three students were entranced by the flying bird, watching its every movement.

As they neared the edge of the forest, the owl flew up and out of the tree tunnel. It was at that moment, returning to reality and ready to speed up again, they all noticed the coughing and sluggishness of the station wagon.

"Oh, what the hell now?" Jess asked. The engine continued to sputter.

The car engine slowly ground to a halt and stopped in a small cloud of dust blown up from the road. Jess tried starting the car several times, but it was no use.

"Well, I guess we're walking," Ben said, obvious depression in his voice.

"You guys can't be serious," said Amanda. "It's gotta be, like, miles from town. We can't walk that far, especially in the dark."

"What, are you scared or something? Afraid an owl might get you? Or a werewolf? Besides, I've got my trusty flashlight." Ben shined the light in both of their faces.

"Okay, we're in the middle of the woods in the middle of the night." Amanda punched Ben in the arm. He had leaned up between the front seats. "We've only got a little flashlight. And that story Mr. Nolan told, it still creeps me out. You're right, I'm scared."

Calmly, Jess stated the obvious. "We don't really have a choice here, unless either of you has a cell phone you haven't mentioned yet. I left mine at home."

"Mine's charging," Amanda said. Why couldn't she have done that yesterday?

"I don't carry one," Ben stated in his matter-of-fact, know-it-all voice. "They cause cancer, you know."

"Your smoking will do you in long before a cell phone could," Jess shot back. Both knew Ben smoked cigarettes, though not in public. He couldn't afford to; his dad was the chief of police and he wasn't yet 18. "Anyway, we're only a little ways from the nearest house. We can walk it from here, call for a tow, and still be back before our parents know we're late. They're expecting us to be out late tonight as it is, with stargazing and all."

With no other option, the three students stepped out of the station wagon, buttoned up their jackets, and started hoofing it down the middle of the county road.

The banks of the dirt road were not quite so steep once you left the woods, and they gradually tapered down to the level of the road as the three students walked between the fields. Eventually a ditch began to form on each side of the road, separating it from the pasture. The grasses were already growing tall in the ditch and under the wire fences at the edge of each meadow. The darkness wasn't complete, and their eyes became more adjusted. To pass the time, they picked out stars and constellations they had learned. That also helped to distract them from the near total darkness and solitude they were in. Their path rose and fell through the hills, and even with their eyes adjusted, they could barely see the wire fences penning in the road. Then they saw the dim lights of a house ahead. It might have been a half-mile, maybe.

All three stopped immediately when they heard the noise. It was like a dog panting. But it was deeper, heavier, like a huge dog that had asthma or something. Ben shined his light in the direction of the noise, but nothing could be seen past the wire fence and the masses of weeds and grasses growing up through the ditch.

"I think maybe we should walk a little faster," Ben suggested after a few moments.

"Let's just go, now." Amanda grabbed the sleeve cuffs of both boys and tugged them forward. They all hurried along the road. The light from the house became a little brighter, but it still seemed like forever away from them. It was like one of those bad movies where you see down the hallway and it stretches away and you never seem to be any closer to the end of it.

Unfortunately, things were not getting any better. The panting noise appeared to be following them. In the still night air they could hear something moving through the grasses in the meadow to their right. Every so often they could hear a deep, low, coughing growl too. They picked up their pace to a near jog.

"Just keep looking straight. Let's keep our cool here. We know we're getting closer," Jess reminded them all. Soon, all they could hear was their footsteps on the hard-packed gravel. Then Ben's light paused.

"It's stopped. The noise, it's stopped. I don't think it's there anymore."

"Well, come on, let's not wait around to find out," Amanda was nearly hysterical now. She certainly hadn't bargained for this when she signed up for astronomy class.

Before they could begin walking again, they started hearing the clicks of footfalls on the road behind them. Whatever it was, it was getting closer, and it had moved out of the field. Amanda couldn't take it anymore. She bolted down the road at top speed. The two boys took a moment to look at each other, and then their resolve broke and they tore off after her. The footsteps continued to pound the hard dirt after them.

***

Tom Watkins, whose family farmhouse was the last on County Road 53 before the state forest, awoke to the kids yelling, screaming, and pounding on his front door. Being a quiet corner of the world, especially at night, most any noise from outside could be heard well, and the loud rapping on the old, solid oak door resounded through the house. He jumped out of bed, pulled on his robe, and tumbled down the stairs followed by his wife. He opened the door and was bombarded by a flying mass of clothing and hair that eventually his mind decided was a teenage girl. In shock, he watched as two other teenage boys plowed inside right after her, nearly knocking him to the floor as they slammed the door shut. The girl had already circled down and around, hugging his waist, finally hiding behind him.

"All right, what's this all about," began Tom, whose surprise had now turned to irritation. The boys were hunched over, trying to recover their breath. The girl had moved on over to Tom's wife and was sobbing uncontrollably while the farm wife comforted her.

"Something out there," Ben stammered between breaths. "Chased us down the road. Had to get inside."

Jess, who was in a little better shape, continued for them. "I'm sorry, mister. We don't mean to bother you. Our car broke down back at the edge of the woods. We were walking up to call for help and we heard something. Some kind of animal, a big animal, and it was growling at us from the field. We tried to just walk fast, but then we heard it following us on the road. The faster we went, the louder it got. Then it growled real loud and we just took off running. It was right behind us, till we got to your yard."

Tom moved to the picture window overlooking the yard and road. The fluorescent outdoor light on his garage lit up the entire area, but there was nothing unusual to be seen.

"Okay, so who are you and what are you doing out here this time of night?" asked Tom.

"I'm Ben Thompson, my dad's the chief of police. This is Jess and Amanda, and we were all out at Lookout Hill with our school class watching the stars. We do that each month, but we've never had a problem before."

"Sounds like you kids got a bit spooked," Tom said after a moment of thought. "Ben, I know your dad. You don't seem to be telling stories here, but you've probably seen a coyote. There are a lot of them around here. Why don't you all call for a ride. I'm going to check out outside."

Tom walked to the end of the living room and opened his handcrafted gun cabinet. He took out a shotgun, loaded it from the drawer on the bottom, and dropped a few extra shells in the pocket of his robe. He then slipped on his farm jacket, stepped into his boots, grabbed an old, heavy flashlight, and walked out onto the creaking porch. He listened carefully, but there was no sound to be heard. He walked across the deck, boards lightly creaking under his weight. His breath wafted out in a white vapor, dissipating in the cold air. Still nothing.

He had lived here for most of his life, and he knew the land and all the creatures on it well. He wasn't afraid of anything, just cautious. If there was a coyote out here, he was determined to keep it from killing any more of his chickens. Tom walked down the steps and across the wet, dewy grass of the front lawn. Within seconds he was under the light of his pole barn looking out at the county road before him. He clicked on the big, metal flashlight and scoured the road. After walking about 20 yards down the county road, he came across some scrapes in the hard-packed dirt. Though there wasn't much definitive to see, his mind thought they did look to be some sort of canine tracks. They show those little claws at the end of the paws when they leave tracks.

He shined his flashlight across the ditch and fields as he heard a lone howl split the night from a long distance away. Coyote, most likely, he thought. And it was heading off away from his farm.

He trudged his way back to the house, eager to get those kids home and return to bed. Obviously their imaginations had gotten the better of them.

***

The three kids weren't about to let the story of their wild night die out on the county road. Before the second hour was over the following morning, word of their encounter with the supposed werewolf was all over school. Fueled by the myth Mr. Nolan told them the previous night, the embellishing of their story took on epic proportions as it passed along the hallways and classrooms, until nearly every underclassman in the building looked at them with awe.

Ben Thompson was quite an intelligent individual, one of the brightest in his class, though his grades didn't always reflect it. He knew there was really something out there, and so he began searching online for any clues as to the creature that had pursued them. It didn't take long to uncover the legend of a beastly canine referred to as the Dogman, which looked like a gigantic wolf yet could stand up on two legs like a human. Several websites had devoted themselves to the explanation and perpetuation of the legend. Though Ben would have normally scoffed at the idea of a werewolf creature running around his town, his recent encounter was enough for him to question his own beliefs. Could this have been a Dogman? Or *the* Dogman? He didn't know for sure, but it was a better explanation than anything else he could come up with. And he could be pretty creative when he needed to be.

On the websites, the eyewitnesses described seeing the creature in various locations in central and northern Michigan. Most accounts were just like those of the three kids. Some described actually sighting the creature, which apparently stood six or seven feet high with glowing yellow eyes and yet a sensation of human intelligence in its countenance. Its behavior varied from being timid and apprehensive, sometimes avoiding and running from human contact, all the way to being aggressive and downright dangerous. There were several unexplained deaths and mysterious disappearances attributed to the contact with the beast.

Ben signed in and included his account of the incident on County Road 53. Privy to information and ruminations from his father, the police chief, Ben surmised his own connections between the unusual events of the past few months and attributed them to the Dogman creature. He added these to his posting. Dozens of responses flooded into his email within days. Ben had unwittingly put Twin Lakes on the crypto-zoological map.

The teachers and adults who heard the story laughed it off as pure imagination. But despite the outrageous claims, the story continued to circulate through town, reaching most of the inhabitants by dinner time.

Werewolves in the woods of Twin Lakes? How absurd was that?

CHAPTER 7

June 2007

The first Monday after school officially let out for the summer, the Twin Lakes police station received a call from the parent of two young boys who had found an abandoned vehicle out in the state forest. It was parked on a short two-track leading down to Crooked Creek. The boys were heading out fishing on Friday afternoon, celebrating school being out and the endless summer vacation finally arriving, when they came upon the van. They didn't think anything about it, other than it was all decked-out, a real customized job. The kids went back out again that Monday, saw it right where it was four days previously, and were a bit suspicious. Really, what would such a nice van be doing out in the sticks anyway? And there wasn't anybody around. They'd fished the area for several hours each day, and they hadn't seen any people around.

And so it was that the two youngest deputies of the Twin Lakes police force, both part-time summer help right out of the academy, were sent out several miles into the state forest to investigate and make a report. Though they were only a few months apart in age, Jake VanPratt, originally from the western side of Michigan, naturally put himself ahead of his partner Mike Smitts, a native of the Upper Peninsula, who was shorter and younger. Jake made Mike drive, and he never tired of telling everyone that he was "chauffeured" everywhere they went.

Of course, the two rookies had heard all the rumors and stories about the strange things happening out here, and they were a bit more inclined to let their imaginations run than their older superiors would. They were extremely cautious when they finally arrived on the scene. Both took a long, slow look out the windows of the police SUV, appraising the situation. There wasn't much to see, just the green foliage of the woods and underbrush, the shadows on the forest floor where the sun's rays didn't poke through, and the rear end of the shiny blue conversion van pulled to the side of the worn two-track. It was actually more of a small motor home than a van, the kind of vehicle a small family could vacation in. While Mike called in the New York license plate, the first from the Empire State they'd seen in the little town since their arrival, his partner stepped out and walked around the abandoned van. The van's driver's side window was down, and Jake, a little suspicious, poked his head inside.

"There's a wallet on the front seat. I'm going to check it out."

"The van is registered to a Douglas M. Wilson of Rochester, New York," called out the driver, who had stepped out of the vehicle and begun walking around the perimeter.

VanPratt paused in his vehicular search and looked over slowly to the younger officer. "You don't mean Doug Wilson, the horror novelist? Let's see if there's some ID."

The older deputy reached in, grabbed the wallet, and found a driver's license. "My God, that's him! I've read most all his books, and his picture's on the back of each one. That's him for sure! I just finished his latest book, *Night Watchers*. It's a vampire special. Lots of blood and gore, just the way I like 'em!"

"I wonder what he was doing way out here?"

"Three guesses, and the first two don't count. I'll bet he was out here thinking he was getting inspired or something from all those wild werewolf stories." Jake snapped his fingers, his eyes wide open. "Maybe he's even researching it a little. I'll bet you a six-pack he's going to write a book about it. Wow, imagine that, us, our little town, actually in a bestseller."

Both officers paused then, lost in the moment. Then they shook off their overactive imaginations.

"Certainly enough stories passed around to give you the impression they're real, you know," Mike said soberly. He was an avid reader of the website postings.

"Yeah, I know what you mean. Let's start with the van, and then work our way around to the woods."

The vehicle was in great condition. Luckily, the last time it rained was the previous week on Wednesday, and there was no sign of water damage to the inside, so they could be sure the van was parked here for five days at the most. Jake opened the vehicle's door and climbed inside. It was a potential bachelor's paradise on wheels. The ceiling had been raised with a custom turtle top, almost giving the deputy room to fully stand. A large leather recliner faced the rear of the van, where a small bench and table held several notebooks and an assortment of pens. A laptop computer lay lazily on its side next to the bench. It was off, probably run out of power days ago. Flies were buzzing around a few empty take-out containers and empty cans of soda on a tiny kitchenette. Above the table in a built-in console were a TV, stereo, and VCR/DVD combo, aptly pointed so they could be seen from the recliner and the bench. What appeared to be a change of clothes was on the floor of the van.

The deputies walked a perimeter of about one hundred yards around the van. The two-track road curved past the vehicles and stopped at a small turnaround campsite a bit ahead. The rustic campsite dropped off and down a steep embankment about 30 feet to the Crooked Creek below. Both officers looked down on the little river, studying the ground around the edge of the precipice, but there was nothing to see there. In fact, there was nothing in the area except for the van, which stood out against the natural world like a sore thumb.

Since they had seen nothing to indicate a struggle, an altercation, or any other kind of unusual activity, the deputies didn't bother to scale down the embankment to the river, where they'd have found the torn remains of a small dome tent and sleeping bag, and several smashed pieces of camping equipment. These were hidden from above, but in plain sight from down at the level of the river bank.

***

The young deputies called in a tow truck to haul the van back to the station. The only tricky action for the driver was backing up a half mile down an overgrown two-track, but the hooking up and towing was easy. Jake and Mike followed it in and then began the ordeal of locating the famous writer and following up on his whereabouts.

After half a day of making long distance phone calls, Jake was finally able to slip through Doug Wilson's massive security net and reach his publicist. A short-tempered woman with a heavy New York accent told the deputy that Mr. Wilson was out of state on sabbatical, researching for a new book. He had left on May 31st, and wasn't due to return until well after July 4th. He could even be later than that. She never bothered to contact the author when he was out in the "wild lands of America digging for his next million," as she so precociously put it. Even his family wouldn't know where he was or expect him to contact them at any regular intervals. He wasn't considered missing, nor would he be missing, until he showed up again ready to work on his next manuscript. She even proceeded to tell the deputy, more in a lecture, that Mr. Wilson had even once disappeared for nearly a year before returning with his completed text tucked under his arm. She chided Jake for bothering her and disrupting her obviously busy day, and hung up on him.

"Guess we were right; he was out researching for a new book. Well, he isn't reported missing by any of his family, friends, or whoever it is he hangs out with," Jake said to Mike, who was sitting on the edge of the desk, "so until someone does miss him, I'm not going to worry about him. With all the summer people and tourists in town now, we have enough to deal with."

***

Later that week, the two boys who had found the van returned to the area to fish once again. They took a much easier means to reach the little creek, avoiding the large embankment and walking along downstream. Their plan had been to head farther downstream, since the fish weren't biting well in this area, their normal fishing hole. However, as luck would have it, they did spot the variety of camping gear, and not making any connection to the vehicle they had spotted earlier in the week, which was gone by this time, they used the various parts to create a fort to play in for the rest of the day. Had they gone a bit farther down stream, they would have undoubtedly found an old Yankees hat, torn and bloodstained, caught on a rock in the creek. But playtime all day in their new fort kept them from exploring. And as their mother always requested, they were home well before sundown for dinner.

***

The so-called experts arrived on the last Thursday of the month, just after noon. The convoy pulled off the highway and crossed over the viaduct into town. A bright shiny green pickup was followed by two large Suburbans, one towing a trailer with several all-terrain vehicles, and the other pulling a long camper trailer. With the exception of the drivers, no other passengers could be seen through the darkly tinted windows. And even the drivers hid their faces behind large sunglasses and baseball caps. At the central stoplight, the vehicles swung right, downtown, and pulled into the small parking lot of the township building. Mid-week was probably the best to avoid the heavy traffic of the thousands of tourists that flocked into town each weekend. But there was no mistaking who they were, and they wanted as much publicity as they could get. They drew the attention of everyone through town, and many tourists and locals alike stopped to gawk, point, and discuss their sudden appearance. The driver of the lead truck casually stepped down and made his way into the quiet cool of the town's offices, his cowboy boots clicking on the pavement and the cement steps. The others remained in their vehicles with the windows up.

A few minutes later, the driver returned to the truck with a large manila packet and a deputy escort, and the convoy fired up its engines again. They followed the officer for two blocks and turned down Second Street, stopping at the village green, where the crew finally emerged from the vehicles and began setting up camp. The deputy pointed out the boundaries of their makeshift campsite, where they could find a few picnic tables, and where to set up their large pop-up canopy tent. The crew worked fast and furiously in a methodical fashion. It was obvious they had done this many times in the past. Walkers through town passed slowly, watching the show. Gawkers were nothing new to the crew; they had set up their camp in dozens of small towns just like Twin Lakes in the past few years. With any luck, they would be able to interview some of these same locals within the next few hours.

Painted in bright golden letters on each vehicle and again on the long camper was the logo of AML, *America's Myths and Legends*. It wasn't every day that one of cable-TV's most highly-acclaimed and recognized shows came to town.

***

AML started out with a bang in its first season. Reggie Bushman, the show's host and an avid outdoorsman, ran the first six shows, as well as the live season finale, from their base camp just outside Yosemite National Park in California. The inaugural season focused on the search for Bigfoot, and Bushman spared no expense in scientific instruments and gadgets. Along with special miniature cameras and microphones that were worn by the crew, satellite tracking devices, GPS units, and a full, yet scaled-down, scientific lab provided the realistic drama of locating, and, according to Bushman, actually capturing a real American myth. His plan was to tag the specimen, track it, and uncover it in the live season-finale episode.

Many videos were taken of the beauty of the California hills and forests, and there were even a few unusual and unexplained sights. Probably the best shot, and the one that extended the show's contract to another season, was a dark shadow moving from one redwood to another along a tree line. Unlike many previous Bigfoot sightings, and even the poor amateur photos and videos, this time the AML crew actually did shoot and tag a creature with a tracking dart, and it was caught on film. The video clearly showed the lurch of the shadow as it was hit by the dart and then tumbled to the ground. Then, amazingly, the creature rolled over, ran on all fours for about 50 feet, and then gracefully rose to continue its escape on two legs. The crew took off after it, tracking with their GPS sensors for nearly two miles before finding the sending units smashed at the base of a large tree along with a splash of blood and tufts of long, stringy, dark brown hair. That video alone, along with the thousands of replays on newscasts and on the internet, was enough to guarantee Bushman's rise to stardom. Analyses of the hair and blood samples were done immediately (and of course on the next show) by the crew at their base camp, and again at a local university laboratory. There were no matches to any known mammal.

Bushman never quite caught his Bigfoot, but he certainly caught the attention of viewers across the country and the world over. After the adventure in California, Reggie took his soon-to-be larger crew (along with several new and expensive scientific gadgets) to New York to search for Champ, the sea serpent of Lake Champlain. The following fall they headed to southwest New Mexico to investigate claims of the infamous blood-sucking Chupacabra. Each season brought higher ratings, more cash, and more help. The crew became celebrities, and the show was famous. Letters and emails begged the show to cover obscure legends all around the country. Eventually Bushman devoted a small section of each show to covering the local flavor. Again, this led to even more viewers and higher ratings as folks watched each week to see if their little community would be featured.

Americans absolutely loved the show, which continued on for another three seasons before attempting to capture northern Michigan's Dogman. The Dogman legend was secondary to a claim of a werewolf creature in southern Wisconsin, but a lack of evidence and the sudden emergence of the northern Michigan stories hitting the internet caught Reggie's attention, and the film crew turned north immediately. This was especially urgent since the legend resurfaced every 10 years, and this was the prime time and the prime spot for an encounter. Reggie knew an opportunity when he saw it, and it was time to cash in before someone else beat him to it.

Reggie Bushman was much more than just an actor. He was also a genius at marketing. By the time he arrived on location, trailers full of t-shirts, sweatshirts, jackets, beach towels, pennants, fridge magnets, and even action figures would be available to the public. He even had many copies of his various books, based on the highly successful campaigns to find America's legendary and mythological beasts. Again, the public just ate it all up. Bushman was counting on a big haul from this summer's tour. The area's normal summer residents, weekend warriors, and influx of tourists added to the huge number of thrill-seekers wanting a glimpse of the adventure of the Dogman myth would provide Reggie with the greatest paying audience he'd ever had.

***

The three AML vehicles were only the first wave of their entourage. This was the advance film and research crew who set up about a month and a half prior to the arrival of the full scientific crew and the actors. The advance team's job was to set up and secure the base camp and prepare all of the equipment for the show. A few members of the team would scour the countryside, researching local archives and interviewing the locals to develop the story. They all had specific jobs to accomplish in what was always a mad rush during the six-week span. Everything needed to be up and running when the bigwigs arrived.

The four-man advance film crew, led by film director Len Hayes, spent the next few weeks filming background shots. Hayes was a tall, slender, pale-skinned man who wore thick, black-rimmed glasses. The essential boss of the crew, and the driver of the front-running green pickup, Len kept them moving all around the county, and then across the state. Their big Suburban scouted the back roads of the county, reverting to the ATVs when the trails became just too narrow for the big rig. They even hired out a local pilot and took several day's film of aerial footage.

Len had been with the show since its inception. He and Reggie were close friends, though they often argued about the artistic rendition of the various shots that were used (and of course left out) of the many episodes. Ultimately it was Reggie's show, so he got his way. Had Len been allowed to use every shot he loved, they'd have to double the length of each season.

The other half of the advance team was the research crew. This group did all the boring book work, often spending days in libraries and damp basements of newspaper offices finding any and all unusual accounts that might relate to the story. After that, they would comb the communities interviewing anybody and everybody they could. Public opinion was huge for developing the story, since the legends were often passed verbally. Often the smallest clue or arcane reference could be embellished into an account in the tale the audience would eventually see. Their job was just as important as the filming itself, and even more hectic because they had so much ground to cover, and so little time in which to do it. Six weeks was never enough, but they slept little and worked long days to pull together the storyline.

Markus Wilkinson, Tim Dillon, and Chad Russell were the three sent to research every strange and unexplainable event in northern Michigan. Their work began by searching online, checking into every discussion group, chat room, and eyewitness report. Then they split up, heading to Muskegon, Traverse City, and Big Rapids to dig through newspaper archives, searching for any evidence that would further explain the legend. All three were young, in their early twenties, eager to spend energetic hours pouring over old documents in the hopes of furthering their careers in the television business. They worked for peanuts, were given free room and board in the various RVs, and most of their paychecks were spent on beer and pizza in the local watering holes.

Graduates of USC, the three had known each other for years as they worked together in many film and tech classes. Of course, growing up in California, they'd seen many strange and unusual sights, and those were just from the strange and unusual people. They loved the AML show as well as their role in its production. But none of the three held much belief in monsters or myths. Human behaviors and beliefs were far more peculiar, mysterious and unpredictable, and were undoubtedly behind the true story of these legends they showed millions on TV each week.

***

Security was obviously going to be a major issue when the full AML staff finally arrived two months later. However, Chief Thompson didn't have an extra deputy he could assign to the traveling circus. The influx of tourists and summer folk kept the normal police staff working overtime as it was, without the extra duties of assisting a major TV production. Even with the extraordinary payment to the township of $1,000 per day for the use of the village green as a base camp, the chief had to look outside his staff to find someone to baby-sit the Hollywood Stars, as the police staff began calling them. On the recommendation of his son Ben, the chief contacted Steve Nolan. Ben had tremendous respect for his mythology teacher. Steve was perfect for the job. He was highly educated in literature, especially myths and legends. He was single and had no summer commitments. He was staying in the area for the next three months until school started again in the fall. And being a teacher, Steve was always looking to supplement his meager earnings.

There was no way Steve could say no, not for the $100 per day the chief was willing to pay for keeping the Hollywood Stars out of his hair. And after meeting Markus, Chad, and Tim, Steve finally had someone his own age to hang out with. Though he loved working with the veteran teachers on his staff, the young researchers provided a welcomed reprieve and an opportunity to spend time discussing mythology with other buffs.

And he was looking for any distraction from his nightmares, which were occurring more frequently and growing more intense with each passing day.

Steve was the first to be interviewed by the team because of his encounter in April while snowshoeing. He'd nearly forgotten it, but the memory came flooding back quickly when he found out they were searching for some wild beast. He really didn't have much to tell them, because he had only heard the howls of an animal, and only three times at that. Mostly it was just a strange feeling he'd had. Steve didn't believe in all of that craziness about a monster out in the woods. He didn't think this was the Dogman they were looking for, but then again, he couldn't exactly say for sure what the animal was. Regardless, his story was taken down as supplemental evidence.

An article in the local weekly newspaper brought in many more locals to tell their story. It was amazing what crawled out of the woodwork. Most accounts were discounted as false sightings and products of the imagination. The USC boys smiled and looked interested, but deep down they weren't impressed by most of the stories. However, each tale was categorized, along with its teller. Most of those interviewed just wanted to a part of the show, asking several times if they were going to be on TV, what should they wear, and when would it be aired, because they wanted to tell all their friends and relatives to watch. Yes, interviewing got old quickly.

Much more interesting to the researchers was the string of unusual events the community had encountered over the past months. These events, by themselves, didn't seem unusual to the townspeople or the police force. But to the USC boys, looking through a fresh, unbiased set of lenses, these various incidents would be the backbone to the story unfolding here in Twin Lakes. Reggie Bushman loved these story lines the best, because they were much more believable than some single, random incident. People could really get into a string of spectacles and believe the story was true.

The unexplained death of Clayton McGowan and the mysterious death of Old Bill Sawyer, along with the missing personage of famous novelist Douglas Wilson (who in three weeks still hadn't shown up to claim his RV from the police parking lot) were far too coincidental to be left out of the story line. Throw in the eyewitness of the redneck family, and even the ramblings of the old insane man, and a great story was in the making.

***

June is an excellent month for fishing in northern Michigan. The weather hasn't turned to the blistering temperatures and still air of August. Nights are often cold and mornings are still cool before the sun warms up the land. The rivers, lakes, and even marshy lands are teeming with pan fish, the bluegills and perch, and the larger fighting fish such as bass, walleye, pike, and muskies, the giant predators of the aquatic world. Fishermen come from all over the country to take a chance at pulling in a monster in the fishing tournaments held in the small towns all over the north.

Don and Tim Turner, brothers who graduated from Twin Lakes High School in the late '70s, continued their love of fishing each year by skipping a day of work in June and July, heading out to the Crooked Creek flooding, their favorite spot since they were young boys.

They always arrived in the very early hours, before the sun rose and wiped away the light foggy mist that always covered and rose over the small, still lake. That old familiar blue had replaced the black sky, and there was just enough light so they wouldn't need a flashlight. They'd row out into the still, mirrored surface, since motors were prohibited on the flooding, and besides, they could slip easily out to the middle without scaring away the fish.

As Don rowed the little 12-foot aluminum craft out, the two sipped some hot coffee from a thermos that Tim always brought. They took their time, as the sun wouldn't come up for another half hour or so. That old familiar blue of the sky slowly began to soften and lighten as they reached their spot, just where a wide inlet poked its way into the woods. The water of the flooding was motionless, and all kinds of water plants were thriving under and on the surface. The DNR always supplied the flooding with small-mouth bass from their hatchery each year, and every June the two brothers usually had no trouble catching their limit by mid-morning. Then they could return to shore, rest easy in their lawn chairs, enjoy a few beers, and enjoy the rest of the day in each other's company, reliving old memories and discussing everything new in their lives. Don lived with his family in Cheboygan, while Tim's family had moved west of Gaylord. Though they weren't really that far apart, their careers rarely gave much time to get together, so they cherished their summer fishing trips. Neither could afford to travel to any exotic location in Canada or out of state, and besides, the Crooked Creek flooding was *their* spot.

They let the little boat drift, not that it was going anyplace soon, and they cast out lines, waiting to see who'd hook up first. The ground fog had lightened up a little, and they could now see bits of the woods, at least from three feet off the ground and up. Within a few moments, their lines were jerking as the pan fish toyed with the lures, and minutes later, both had brought in bass, though Don's was an inch too short, so he released it back into the wild. He'd certainly get another chance; the fish were really hitting this morning. All signs were pointing to an excellent day.

That is, until the fish suddenly disappeared. Minutes drifted by with no action at all. What had seemed to be an excellent start was marred by a light splashing sound coming from the bank of the flooding, opposite of where they had parked their trucks and launched the boat. Neither man could see what created the commotion because of the fog, but they did notice it was getting nearer. They reeled in their lines slowly and quietly, listening to whatever it was coming closer and closer to their boat.

Tim spotted it first, a dark shape in the mist a little above the water coming toward them. Though the fog diminished most of its features, he had no problem telling what it was, or what it resembled anyway. "It looks like a dog, Don. Hey, pooch, what are you doing way out here? Are you lost?" he called toward the animal. "There must be someone else out here fishing too."

But Don's eyesight was better than his brother's, and he noticed what his brother missed right away. It wasn't a dog that was swimming out to them. Though it was paddling like a dog would in water, its head wasn't like any dog Don had ever seen. Its muzzle wasn't long enough, and it was sort of wrinkled up, revealing long, curved fangs that almost seemed to be smiling at them across the water. The hair on its head was slicked back from the soaking water. Though it was a good 30 feet away, it bridged that gap in a few seconds, almost before the two brothers could react.

What finally put Tim into motion was the creature's yellow eyes. They were glowing in some unearthly way as it reached the boat and, quite un-dog like, reached up its *hands*, not paws, and grasped the edge of the little boat, its claws scraping the metal. Good God, it was trying to get into the boat with them! As it tried to heave itself up, it gave out a throaty growl, unlike any animal either had ever heard before. That was all it took for Tim to grab an oar, wind up like a major leaguer, and swing for all he was worth. It would have been a deep one into left-center. The stout oak paddle connected with a direct hit diagonally from the creature's upper cheek across its face and muzzle. The monster howled in pain, removing one hand (paw) from the boat to grasp its wounded head. The sound of its agony pierced both men to the center of their being. Tim didn't wait for the monster to react, and swung the paddle down again on its claws, still holding fast to the boat. A sick crunch emerged from its paw as the edge of the paddle pinched the stout hairy fingers between itself and the metal edge of the gunwales. The creature's second howl of pain was cut short as it slipped off the boat and submerged.

That was all the time the brothers needed, as Don had already been frantically paddling away back toward their trucks during the battle. Tim joined him and the little boat swung around, nose pointed to the shore and their safety. The water broke about 15 feet away now, and the creature again split the air with its painful howls. But then after a few seconds it refocused itself and began swimming after the boat, snarling the entire time, anger fused with its pain.

Luckily the two brothers had a good lead on the creature, and their combined strength allowed them to move across the still water much faster than their pursuer. They could glide quickly while its bulk was dragged by dog-paddling. However, it was not giving up. Even through the fog, which was still slowly lifting, they could see its head and muscular shoulders propelling it through the water. Now they could see the bank, and their vehicles a hundred feet away.

"We take your truck," Tim said to his brother, out of breath from the exertion. "You're closest to the road out. Forget mine, we'll come back for it later."

"I'm with you. Leave the boat too," Don replied, also between breaths. "Let's just get out of here."

Fifty feet, 25 feet, 10 feet, and then the little boat beached itself on the bank. The brothers scrambled out, leaping clear of the water and sprinting to Don's truck. They could still hear the creature swimming furiously behind them, getting ever closer.

The two reached the truck, which was luckily unlocked, and then paused for what seemed the longest few seconds of their lives as Don fumbled in the pockets of his jeans for the key. Tim looked back, shaking a bit from the encounter. He'd never seen anything like it. At long last, Don had the key out, both clambered in, and the truck rumbled to life. The rear-view mirror showed Tim the creature reaching the little boat, and as the truck tore off down the little two-track, he saw it emerge from the flooding, water dripping down its furry legs. Then it really hit him. The creature wasn't down like an animal; it was standing up on its back legs.

That was the last either saw of the creature. Though they returned a few hours later in the heat of the sunny day to reclaim Tim's truck and the boat, this time they were heavily armed. They took off, going their separate ways back home. Neither reported the incident, even after they started hearing more stories and rumors the rest of the year. Though they still got together on a semi-regular basis, neither would ever bring up the incident again. But no longer would they ever return to fish in the Crooked Creek flooding. Their summer trips were always to places a little more populated from that year on.

CHAPTER 8

July 2007

J uly marks the height of the tourist season in the northern tip of Michigan. Well before the 4th, the summer folk have opened up their summer cabins and cottages, re-stocked the pantries with proper staples, snacks, and booze for unexpected (and sometimes uninvited) guest dinners and Sunday barbecues, and pulled the boats and jet-skis up along their weathered docks. Most of the summer folks keep to themselves, enjoying the warm breezes blowing over the heavenly bluish-green water of Carson Lake or Long Lake. These are the people with old money. They hang around their expensive homes relaxing, playing bridge, visiting with old neighbors, and dining out at the fancy restaurants at night. They are a different breed altogether compared to the tourists.

The tourists, or "fudgies" as the locals call them, on the other hand, speed up north every Friday night, battling heavy traffic on the expressway in order to have as many minutes of fast-paced fun as they can cram in a weekend until they have to speed back home on Sunday. These people haul up their speedboats and ATVs and jam-pack the stores and tourist traps, spending money like it's going out of style. They buy out the markets' stock of beer, regardless of the brand (and the local stores keep plenty of cases of the lower-end brands, marked up to make a nice profit). The tourists couldn't care less about the high prices they're paying to fill the gas tanks of their showy SUVs and recreational vehicles. They want the "up-north" experience, but they still want it to fall under their high-paced lifestyles.

July brings the many celebrations designed to rake in those precious tourist dollars. The July 4th holiday kicks off the month with its parade of kids throwing candy and an elaborate fireworks display, which is quite extensive for a little town with a little budget. Old-fashioned days, two weeks later, takes visitors back in time with an antique car and tractor show, pie bake-offs, a chili cook-off, and games like sack races for the kids. And finally, at the end of the month, residents brace themselves for the great Tip of the Mitt Powerboat Races, the largest event of the summer. This weeklong event begins on Wednesday with the arrival of the boaters, who spend two days in time trials and two nights in the beer tent downtown. The race was once even filmed on a cable sports channel, though the show was run a month later during the graveyard shift and few locals were able to watch it. The races themselves stretch from the northern tip of Carson Lake down through the Bear River and up to the northern tip of Long Lake, just before the Cheboygan River. Racers make a round trip, and because of the staggered starts, the little high-speed boats pass each other in the dangerous and narrow tight corners of the Bear River. The locals love to pull up their pickups and lawn chairs and sit on the edge of the river, drinking beers and waiting (and sometimes hoping) for a collision to liven up the weekend. Most years, they aren't disappointed, as one of the tiny boats will lose control and slam into a seawall. A few years back, two boats smashed into each other with disastrous results.

The month of July is vital to the economy of northern Michigan, and to Twin Lakes in particular. It is the one month that most of the locals will stake their livelihoods, their yearly incomes, on, making enough in those four or five weeks to last over the winter. Twin Lakes has no industry, and few large employers, and those are tied to the summer visitors in some fashion anyway. The tourist dollars keep the whole area afloat. July has the best weather of the summer months. June is still a bit cool, and there is still work to be done in the nine-to-five jobs down in the cities to the south. August is far too hot, and the vacationers hide out all day on the water, not spending money in the stores. But July is just right. The bright green grass on the fairway is clipped short. The leaves on the majestic oaks and maples are large and rippling in the breeze, and provide plenty of shade. The little smooth pebbles stand out against the tan, hard-packed sandy lake bottoms, easily seen through the crystal-clear water. Yes, everyone's ready for a vacation in northern Michigan in July.

***

Ron and Marge St. Andrews had been working on their rustic, woodsy cabin for nearly a year now. Their dream of an up-north getaway became closer with each weekend they could spend in Twin Lakes. Marge, a stay-at-home wife, spent many of her days planning out each vital step in the cabin's construction, everything from the structural design to the layout of heating, cooling, and plumbing systems. She had finished her degree in architecture from U of M in 1972, but gave it up when she married Ron, who had just accepted an extremely high-paying job as an electrical engineer. There was no reason for her to work, as Ron quickly moved up the professional ladder, and she could concentrate on her role as mother to their two children.

They bought the five-acre plot five years ago, just before the land prices up north boomed. Ron saved a large chunk of his engineer's salary over that time period to put into their building project. The land was situated just a mile or so east of the freeway, just south off of Townline Road. Their property backed up to the edge of the Crooked Creek State Forest, so their five acres actually afforded them even more privacy than they could afford.

Since the cabin wasn't finished, the two had been camping out in their snowmobile trailer. Ron and their two boys often traveled north over the past dozen winters to snowmobile through the trails. They couldn't afford a true motor home or even a camper while saving up all their resources and their snowmobile trailer was more than big enough to hold an inflatable mattress at night. They had even rigged up a light at the ceiling so they could play cards at night. Plus, the trailer did double duty, each weekend hauling all of the tools, lumber, and supplies the couple needed to work on their retirement cabin.

They didn't go into town much, and so they missed all of the gossip about the mysterious events supposedly going on in the state forest.

After working all day and well into the evening, Ron and Marge relaxed over a couple of games of cribbage before their tired bodies finally demanded rest. They had just settled down to sleep in the makeshift comfort of their trailer when a loud crash startled them back to consciousness. Even through the aluminum walls of the trailer they could recognize the sounds as emerging from their unfinished cabin. Somebody was rummaging around in their soon-to-be vacation home.

Ron was up in a flash, and pulled on his jeans and red fleece jacket moments later. He slipped his bare feet into his work boots without lacing them up and grabbed the closest flashlight.

"Honey, it's late and dark. Are you really going out there?" Marge asked.

"Of course I am. If some redneck's out there, I'm sure as hell not going to let them screw up any of our work or steal any of our tools."

They had dealt with two incidents over the past months involving break-ins. First somebody had taken off with a new air compressor they had innocently left between weekends. After that, they always packed up all of their belongings before returning home on Sunday evening. A few weeks later there had been a bit of vandalism, the charred remains of a campfire, and a pile of beer cans. Ron and Marge could easily guess what caused that.

"Well, let me go with you at least."

"No, you stay here. I'll deal with this. It's probably the same kids who were partying here a few weeks ago. I'll put an end to this nonsense, so help me."

Ron stepped outside the little side door of the trailer and shined the light ahead over the unfinished yard and driveway. Only 30 feet away he could see the nearly completed shell of the cabin. They had paid a local contractor to put up the foundation, the exterior walls, and the roof, but basically everything else they were going to construct themselves. The window openings were covered in translucent plastic that flapped in the light breeze, and the front doorway was covered over by a blue tarp. There were no lights inside that Ron could see. He flashed his light around the clearing that would become their front yard. There were no vehicles here, nor down the driveway that he could see. Whoever it was had hiked back here.

Another loud crash from inside the cabin drew Ron's attention. He knew exactly the sound of a pile of two-by-fours tumbling to the floor. Cautiously he strode up to the covered front doorway, then lifted the tarp slowly with his flashlight and peered inside. A few moments later, having seen nothing immediately in the front lower level, he climbed the two makeshift cinderblock steps, temporary until their porch was finished, and entered the cabin.

Marge, of course, couldn't just sit tight. She clicked on the overhead light, dressing quickly as soon as her husband had left the trailer, and stepped out into the cold summer night. A quarter moon was rising just above the treetops and would soon shine brightly down into the clearing. Already much of the ground was visible in the moonlight. Only a few scattered and puffy clouds mingled up above, catching the moon's light, their top edges glowing gray against the deep blue-black sky. Many stars were out, far more than Marge would ever see from their home in the midst of the city. The light breeze shook the branches at the very top of the trunks, the leaves whispering and chattering as they rubbed against each other. All in all, it was a beautiful night. But she couldn't help but shiver, knowing somebody, or some *thing*, was out here messing with their up-north dream house. True, it was a cabin, and not a real house, but she loved thinking of it in that way.

Not more than three feet from the trailer, she stared at the cabin, waiting patiently for her husband to return. She pulled her flannel shirt-jacket a little tighter around her torso, hugging her arms around herself. What was taking him so long?

Ron had crept silently through the front room of the cabin, still hearing noises far to the rear of the building. Somebody was definitely in here. The noises were far too loud to be created by some little critter. Things were being knocked about, as if somebody was searching for something, and making a mess while doing it. Ron thought about those mystery movies where some Mafia guys would thoroughly turn over an unsuspecting victim's apartment. He shined the light around and spotted a left-over chunk of a two-by-two, about four feet long and just the right size to grip tightly in his right hand. He picked it up, much more grateful to have some sort of weapon to use if necessary. He reached the framed-in hallway leading to the kitchen, bath area, and back bedrooms, stepping over and around several piles of lumber and scraps that had been knocked helter-skelter around the room. Gathering his courage, he raised his weapon as he shined the light down the hallway, and called out, "Whoever's down there, come out. This is my place, and you need to get out right now." For good measure, he added, "I've already called the cops, and they'll be here any minute."

Ten seconds ticked by with no answer, though for Ron it felt like minutes. The crashing and banging had stopped when he hollered down the length of the cabin. An uneasiness grew in the man. Again, he called out, "Whoever's there, I'm giving you one last warning." The answer returned before his last word was finished. A low, menacing growl echoed through the house. Ron froze, the hair on his back and neck standing straight up. A pair of little lights had turned on at the back end of the hallway, about 20 feet away. Ron stared at them, entranced, until they blinked. Now it was his eyes that widened. He started backing up, but noticed the glowing yellow eyes were moving steadily down the hallway toward him.

Ron panicked. This was no vagrant hiding out, nor some kids trying to party down in his house. Whatever it was, it wasn't human. He turned to run out of the building, but stumbled over a pile of lumber, knocking wooden boards in all directions. Though he didn't know it at the time, nor could he appreciate his clumsiness at the moment, his fall actually saved his life. The creature darted forward, closing the gap in two massive leaps, and was through the doorway when a pair of two-by-fours, jettisoned upward in Ron's trip, clubbed the monster on either side of its face. The boards were luckily angled just enough to smart the creature on the bridge of its snout, just below its eyes. The creature, off balance in mid-air, crashed just to the left of the man who was already scrambling to right himself.

In the darkness, the creature jerked its head back, blinking its eyes rapidly. Then it sneezed once, twice, three times, spraying Ron and the room in sticky, elastic goo. Each sneeze rocked its head back, and it actually fell over on the final convulsion. That was enough for Ron to rise up and swing his right hand back, firing the two-by-two rod he'd been wielding. It hit the creature in the belly, nearly knocking the wind from its chest.

The creature shook off the injury in seconds and turned its attention to the tarp flapping over the main doorway. Ron had blasted through it in his mad dash to escape.

Marge had heard her husband call out into the depths of the cabin. He's so brave, she had thought. Then she heard the awful growl, and nearly peed her pants. Her feelings immediately changed to unbridled fear as she worried for her husband's safety. She took another few steps toward the house, unsure about what to do. She was caught between the basic instinct to flee and hide and the more difficult decision to move forward and help her husband. Then the loud clatter of boards froze her in her tracks. She waited impatiently for a few seconds, absolutely sure something awful was happening to Ron.

Then the tarp blew open unexpectedly and a dark shape exploded into the clearing. It surprised her so much she nearly fell over backward. It hit the ground and rolled, popping back up as it tore off in her direction. Only then did she realize it was Ron. He was waving his arms, shouting, "Get in the trailer, now!" Half a moment later another larger black form erupted from the house, this one wearing the tarp. Only that wasn't quite right. It had ripped nearly through the blue plastic that covered the doorway, its shoulders and arms tugging desperately to free itself as it bounded after Ron. It was some sort of animal, its wolf-like head clearly visible in the moonlight. Its eyes glowed a bright yellow, and she could see the fangs clearly in its muzzle. This was a nightmare, right out of a horror movie. But this was really happening. That was finally enough to break her from the spell.

Marge jumped into the trailer, quite a feat for a woman her age. A moment later Ron was inside, trying to pull the door tightly behind him. She rolled over, sure she'd twisted her ankle, and watched as Ron tugged on the door handle, just fractions of an inch from closing it tight. But she couldn't figure why it wouldn't completely shut. He kept pulling and tugging, and she then realized he was battling the creature. Her eyes opened wide as she realized their fate if they couldn't keep it out. The tug continued. Despite the pain in her ankle, she jumped up looking to help in any way possible.

Ron continued to strain with all he had, and Marge noticed several hairy fingers clutching the door and preventing it from closing fully. Except they weren't exactly fingers. They were more like claws, each with a long, sharp nail at its end. She looked around frantically, and grasped a tire iron from the floor. While her husband pulled, Marge swung the heavy end of the tire iron, smashing the creature's black claws against the inside of the door. A howl of pain, shock, and rage reverberated through the little trailer. She swung again and heard the sickening crunch of bones shattering. The clawed fingers popped back and Ron slammed the door shut, locking the pin bolt.

They both were gasping for breath, Ron with his hands on his knees and Marge standing with the tire iron like some deranged minor league batter. Ron looked up at his wife, and between gasps, smiled and chuckled at her appearance. Half-heartedly, she smiled back. They'd done it!

Their moment of relief was shattered as a tremendous force slammed into the side of the trailer. Both were knocked to the floor as again and again the creature tried to bash its way in. The two could see the metal sides of the trailer bend in with each blast, but it held together. The onslaught stopped for a few seconds, and then they felt the monster land with a dull thud on the roof. This gave more easily than the sides, denting in as the creature jumped and bounded on it from above. But again, though the ceiling did push down a foot or so, it held and wouldn't burst open. Ron and Marge huddled together like frightened children in the center of their sardine can as the assault continued for nearly a half-hour. Luck was again on their side, as the trailer had no windows to smash, and the back drop-down tailgate was up and latched securely. Despite all of the creature's savage attempts, it just couldn't break in. Finally, mercifully, the attack stopped, and an unsettling silence crept over the scene.

The couple didn't move for hours, clutching each other tightly just like two little, frightened children. They fell asleep in each other's arms, not in passion or lust, but out of fear and exhaustion.

Hours later, the sun shined down brightly through the tree branches, but the truck and the trailer were nowhere to be seen. The only noise to be heard was from the translucent plastic flapping in the light breeze that flowed through the unfinished cabin. The blue tarp lay in shreds about halfway between the building and the driveway. The site had been completely abandoned.

Later that week in the residential section of the local paper was an ad for a five-acre property and half-finished cabin for sale. It offered *"A dream location for a hunting camp or up-north get-away home. All offers would be seriously considered."*

***

Tim, Markus, and Chad met back at the base camp with Steve on July 30. The full contingent of the AML staff was due to arrive in four days, and they had only a few hours to pull together their various findings into a complete history of this legendary beast. They had to coordinate their research with the film footage Len Hayes' crew had taken. After all of the local flavor had been thoroughly documented and added to the findings from across the state, a true legend was arising.

A large map of Michigan had been posted on a cork board. Dozens of little colored pushpins were stuck in the paper, indicating the locations of stories, sightings, and even attacks. The four young men stared long and hard at the map before the discussion began.

Chad started the conversation. "Alright, let's start by checking out these news accounts I pulled from the Traverse City and Muskegon newspapers. These accounts go back nearly a hundred years, and are from all over the central and west side of the state." He handed copies all around. "Just listen to these:

"1997—In Kingsley through the spring, a number of farmers reported small livestock missing, everything from chickens to sheep to piglets, and even an old cow. Eyewitness reports tell of a large wolf that was seen several times on the outskirts of the town, always lurking around the various farms and ranches. It is also reported being seen passing through a scout camp by a group of boys canoeing down the Boardman River.

"Summer of '97, road crews operating outside Rapid City find many unusual signs as their work progresses. They reported large claw marks in trees and on road signs, sightings of a large, dark predator lurking in the shadows just barely visible in the woods.

"In the fall, strange howls were heard around the town of Ellsworth over a week's time. Residents of the Chain of Lakes reported seeing fewer deer during hunting season than normal. No ideas surfaced for the poor deer harvest. Even the Department of Natural Resources was baffled, since the farmlands and orchards of Antrim County are traditionally a hotbed for deer.

"1987—Several incidents of vandalism occurred in Grand Traverse and Benzie Counties over a year's span, including claw marks all over the front doors of a rural church. There were numerous sightings by campers, residents, and concert-goers at the local venues, along with several missing persons, traces of whom have not been found since. Most details are very sketchy.

"1977—A break-in at a hunting cabin between the villages of Leroy and Luthor in the early spring. There were dog-like tracks all around in the soft ground. But they were quite a bit larger than any ever seen before, and that was documented by a DNR officer. Claw marks were scratched in a quarter of an inch into the old, thick oak siding as high up as seven feet above the ground. A number of personal articles were strewn around the cabin, but no witnesses and no contact with its owners. It's as if they just disappeared off the face of the earth.

"Over the summer of '77 campers and fishermen at Claybank Lake, as well as residents of the town of Manistee report eerie howling in the wilderness.

"In September, a group of tourists staying in a cabin near Bear Lake reported a gigantic, dog-like creature with intense, glowing eyes, looking in their windows. They left in a hurry the next morning.

"1967—Three Central Michigan University students ventured out into the woods and fields of Weidman, a farming community west of Mount Pleasant. Based on a story they heard a fellow student tell, the three waited at the side of an abandoned barn until they saw something walk out of the nearby woods on all fours and then stand up and lope around the field on two legs. When they were spotted, the creature chased after their car, keeping pace as they watched the speedometer reach upwards of 40 miles per hour. They couldn't go any faster because of the winding trails they were following. The student in the backseat said he could see the creature's face and glowing yellow eyes , but wouldn't give more details. He was scared even a month later when he was interviewed. Finally, they lost it when they reached the paved county road.

"In 1957..."

Steve had let his mind wander. He hated to think that this all could be dramatized and glamorized by Hollywood. Deep down, he always wanted to believe in the myths, legends and folklore he so often taught his students. Sure they were outrageous and outlandish, but they generally spoke to a simpler time in human existence. Not for the first time did he wish he could leave the modern world behind and live in the realm of mythology.

"A 1937 account, outside Paris, in Mecosta County, on the banks of the Manistee River, a man out fishing was accosted by several wild dogs. He pulled out a revolver and fired the pistol into the air to scare them off. They bolted, but the last one, which was also the biggest one, stood upright on its back legs just like a human and looked him in the eye. Before it bounded away, it grinned at him in a most peculiar way.

"In 1927..."

It was too much for Steve, all these events over all these years. Some were innocent sightings, and others had tragic results. He wondered how many other incidents there were, unreported, that would remain unknown. He wondered how many missing people would never be found. And were they connected to this legend? His daydreaming took him back to his nightly visions of running through the dark forest, bounding effortlessly over logs and rocks, always feeling he was searching for something. There was something just out of his reach, some part of himself that he needed to reclaim. He couldn't rest until it was found.

"But the best story," Chad added, "is the oldest one. It's from an old fur-trader's journal that Markus acquired, and describes what might be the first attack. The creature pursued him and his companions for miles down river before ambushing them. The author barely escaped, though he was sure he could sense the creature following him, and over several months he finally returned back to Fort Mackinac. The encounter left him with horrible dreams for the rest of his life. He even thought he was the beast in his dreams."

That caught Steve's attention. It wasn't possible, was it? He'd never revealed his own dreams to anyone, not his parents, not his friends. Was it possible he was connected to the story? It was just too coincidental.

Chad finished up. "There are plenty of sightings here, tracing back a long way. Granted, the further back you go, the more sketchy the accounts. And some years seem to have more sightings and events than others. But the clippings do demonstrate the 10-year pattern of appearances. I have no idea why that is, and I can't find any reason why."

"So, if we were to analyze your data, assuming of course that this creature is real, or real enough for our legend that we have legitimate sightings, what are we seeing?" asked Markus.

"It seems a bit obvious that there are years in which the sightings are scattered all around, even up to a 60-mile radius," replied Chad. "So, unless there are several of these creatures running around in the north woods, and capable of traveling great distances in a short amount of time, we can eliminate a few of the sightings as bogus."

Tim, who had been with the show the longest, always looked for the wildest story. "Of course, the boss man would probably rather use the multiple monster angle in the overall story plot, but who knows?"

Anything to increase the TV ratings and sell merchandise. The USC boys had listened to Reggie lecture them all the time about embellishing the story, stretching it as far as possible to get the most out of it.

"Okay, so what else do we have here?" Steve asked. He mind was back and focused, and he was really getting interested.

"Well, there are also years where the sightings are concentrated around a particular area, staying within a very tight radius," Chad stated. "I'd think these are the more likely, though of course you have the mass hallucination concept."

The three researchers had seen that before. Tim affirmed what they had all been thinking. "Yeah, one person thinks he sees something, and his neighbors, not to be outdone, also start seeing things. Talk about keeping up with the Joneses." These particular versions tended to bring out the most outlandish stories. Of course, Tim loved them.

Steve had been studying the map carefully. "All I see is sightings basically south of M-72. So why is the creature way up here in Twin Lakes? I mean, for nearly 80 years, the sightings are in the rough geographical area of the central and western part of the state. What has brought the myth this far north?"

"I was wondering that too," responded Tim. "And after digging through the state population demographics online, I thought about how people have settled in the state. In the early to mid-1900s, the west side of the state was pretty much as wild and unsettled as it was up north. In many ways, the north was even more populated. Look at the region around Petoskey, for example. Tourists have traveled there for over a century to treat their allergies. Yeah, hard to believe, but true. There were even ritzy camps in the area and a train to connect them to the steamships in Petoskey and Traverse City.

"So, as the population has been increasing in the west side of the state, of course more houses were built, the cities and towns have gotten bigger, and more and more of the wilderness has been tamed. But the northern tip of the peninsula has maintained its wilderness. I'd say it's a natural for a wild animal to continue to move away from the population and try to maintain its natural habitat, whatever that may be in this case."

"Maybe there's another explanation," Chad said quietly. The others looked over at him as he was studying a Michigan road atlas. "Maybe it's heading north for a reason. Maybe it's looking for something. Or following something."

Steve thought again about his dream, that strange feeling that a search was taking place. Something was taken and must be reclaimed. Still, he held back from the group.

"Okay, now I've got you all beat," boasted Markus smugly. "I've had the rare opportunity to personally sit down with a local native and hear first-hand about the history of the myth."

"You did what?" asked Chad.

"I found an old guy through a contact at the Traverse City paper. His name is Joseph Blackford, he traces his ancestry back through the Ottawa nation. He has been collecting stories about the Dogman for decades, and comparing them to legends of his people. Though he didn't want anything to do with being on TV, he was very helpful in sharing his findings with me.

"You see, there are shape-shifters and then there are shadow-walkers. Shape-shifters are humans who bond with an animal token or icon, and can become like that animal. You hear about these in all sorts of Indian legends all over the country. Those are the coming-of-age stories, you know, the ones where the young brave sets out in the wilderness, makes a connection with some sort of a spirit-animal, and returns to the village as a man. In times of trouble or difficulty in life, the spirit-animal guides the man, and so forth.

"There are even stories where the natives physically became their honorary animal. Probably the most famous are the Dog-Soldiers of the Cheyenne. These were the warriors that fought the US Cavalry for all those years out in Wyoming and the Dakotas. They believed they had the ability to bring out their animal's traits in themselves, becoming very fast, cunning, and voracious enough to outwit and even defeat far more powerful opponents. There were even reports of U.S. soldiers who thought they saw the Indians running on all fours, and changing into canine creatures. A bit far-fetched, I know, but hey, we're in the Hollywood business. The show needs these angles to sell the overall story.

"Now, what I've gathered is this: Shape-shifters seem to be awful, but they are actually just tricky spirits. They're out for fun and games, they're silly sometimes, and can be vengeful sometimes, though they aren't usually malicious.

"Then, there are these shadow-walkers. These, I learned, are believed to be demons that have entered the world by some magical means. They also have the ability to shape-shift, but they are the worst of the worst. These are actually quite popular in the literature and legend of native people. Many tribes in the east and here in Michigan talk of the Windigo, for example, a forest spirit that can take the form of a gigantic part-human, part-bear-like creature. It soars through the woods in a blast of power and can level entire villages.

"These stories are all over the Upper Midwest. The Ioway Indians of Iowa, for example, believed in a wolf-like animal they named "shunka warak'in," which translates to mean "carrying-off dogs." These Indians claimed that the "shunka warak'in" would come into their villages at night and steal children. The beast could walk upright and use its front paws just like arms."

The young men sat there, silent for a few moments. Though none of them implicitly believed in the wacky stories and myths, they each, deep down in the core of their being, often wondered about the truth behind the story, even if it was very slim.

"And the old Indian just told you all this?" Chad asked.

"Yeah, though I did buy him lunch. He even gave me the little journal he'd uncovered a few years back. It was the only real, documented, historical encounter with the beast. That's where Chad and I found that ancient story. It was the best 12 dollars I've spent in ages."

Finally, Steve asked the question they were all thinking. "Okay, so if this is the case, which do we have here, a shape-shifter or a shadow-walker?"

"How should I know? I just do the research, man. It's up to the big boss and the writers to pull it together. Even old Joseph wasn't sure, because so little existed about any of the sightings. But if I had a guess, and if these things were actually real, I'd put my money on the shadow-walker. Far too many deaths and disappearances that could be deaths are going on in this place. I'm surprised no one has taken it seriously yet. You'd think the FBI would have a file on this or something."

"You always play the devil's advocate. It wouldn't hurt you for once to try to believe in one of our shows."

"Why? We hardly ever find anything resembling evidence on any of these monsters. You yourself know the show's mostly good music, special effects, camera angles, and a lot of scientific crap that no one watching will understand anyway."

Steve had leaned back in his chair, a bit out of the conversation. His mind was a whirl of crazy thoughts. A historical fur trader who'd first encountered the beast. This man lived in the Mackinac area, where Steve's ancestors lived. He shared the same dreams of being the beast. Could Steve even be the creature? No, it wasn't possible. But he was tied to the legend; of that he was becoming more sure each day. Steve found himself dozing off listening to the three researchers assembling the history of the Dogman legend that would become the backbone of this fall's most watched TV show.

CHAPTER 9

August 2007

The slivered edge of the axe sliced through the hot summer air and embedded itself an inch deep in the oak log. Even though Jake was only 13 years old, he could chop wood with the best of 'em. He'd been helping his father since he was six, and had graduated up to splitting logs into firewood when he received his own axe on his tenth birthday. Each log was split in half, and then each half was sectioned into manageable pieces that would fit in their home's woodstove.

Young Sammy, who just turned eight, was too little to be using the woods tools, so he was in charge of hauling the split logs over to the old Dodge pickup. He could carry three or four at a time, tossing them up over his head and into the truck's bed. Later on after a few trips, he'd climb in back and stack them up neatly so they could get as many in as possible. His older brother had shown him the right way, and he'd learned it from his daddy. Jake and Daddy were his biggest role models and heroes, so whatever they said he took it to heart.

Andrew Bierstone took a break, shutting down his chain saw, removing his gloves, and wiping the sweat from his brow and neck. It was always awful cutting wood in the heat of the summer. He tried to go out in the later afternoon, when the sun was on its way down and the extreme high temperatures of the day were at least tapering. Not that it made it much more bearable. The exertion of forcing the saw through the dense wood, over and over, and then dragging the heavy logs over to his oldest son would break sweat even on a cold day.

Andrew marched his slim, five-nine frame over to the large stump they'd used as a snack table and pushed aside their three woods jackets, opening up their little camping cooler. The stump table was their catch-all while they were out, with extra clothing, tools and parts they may need, and Sammy's little toys strewn around it. He rummaged past a few bologna and cheese sandwiches and removed a plastic two-liter soda bottle, taking a long swig of cold water. They didn't have enough money to buy those fancy bottled waters at the Trading Post. So, his wife filled up an empty soda bottle with good old tap water, stuck it in the freezer for a bit, and voila! He'd have cold refreshment when he and the boys were out working. Not that it compared with a cold brew on a day like today, but that'd wait till he got home.

He watched the two boys, who were working efficiently. Jake split the logs with precision, and Sammy organized the piles for a maximum load. Andrew was very proud of his two sons. He didn't even have to be right there for them to do what they were supposed to do.

Another swig of water later, Andrew found himself looking around at the beauty of the state forest. The sun was setting, though there was still enough daylight to work for another half hour before heading home. He'd grown up here in Twin Lakes, and appreciated the outdoors and simple lifestyle. He'd learned to cut wood with his father in these woods when he was a lad. And now it had come around full circle.

All three stopped in their tracks when they heard the low howl echo through the forest. Andrew immediately turned his attention to the kids, who were staring off into the trees.

"Daddy, what's that?" asked Sammy, apprehensively. It was obvious the noise had unnerved him.

Andrew walked over to the boys and put his hand on Sammy's shoulder. "Probably just a coyote. There's nothing to be scared of, son. They don't get anywhere near people. And besides, it sounded a ways away. Let's get a move on, we're almost done for the night."

The three resumed their chores. Andrew returned to knock down two more trees he'd spied earlier. The boys went back to their jobs, though they spent more than a few moments looking off into the woods around them.

Jake had just split up another oak log when the howl came again, this time much louder and closer. The hair stood up on the back of his neck. When he looked over at Sammy, their expressions matched each other: eyes widened in fear, the corners of their mouths pulled back. Sammy had dropped his load of firewood. Whatever it was, it was something to be afraid of.

The two boys skittered to each other, backing up to the passenger side door of the truck. Their eyes darted around the forest looking for the source of the noise.

Andrew was still cutting up the last tree and hadn't heard the creature. Fortunately, he looked up to catch sight of his boys and saw them cowering beside the truck. As soon as he shut down his chainsaw, the howl came again.

That was when Jake spied the creature. It was a black blur about 50 yards into the forest. Though he'd never seen a bear in the wild, that was the only animal his mind could possibly register. It was moving easily and at a leisurely pace through the underbrush. Jake was mesmerized by the creature, until it stopped, looked right at him with glowing yellow eyes, and let out a bloodcurdling growl.

Andrew spun at the sound, stared at the creature, and the chainsaw dropped to the ground. Years of being in the outdoors didn't prepare him for the appearance of this monstrous beast. It sure wasn't something he'd ever seen before. It wasn't a bear, and it wasn't a wolf, though it seemed to have characteristics of both creatures. His top priority was to get his children to safety. Even before he turned to run back to the truck, he hollered for them to climb inside and lock their door. A few seconds later he was in the cab, holding and comforting them with the doors securely locked. Unfortunately, they couldn't go anyplace because the truck keys were in the pocket of Andrew's jacket, lying a ways away on the stump.

The creature sauntered into the clearing about 20 yards away, moving gracefully on all fours. It was sort of like a wolf, but covered completely in pitch black, thick and shaggy fur. It had a long snout and tall ears that pointed straight upwards. Now that it was fully visible, it certainly wasn't as bulky as a bear, though its rear hips were large and high. It sniffed the ground as it walked, occasionally looking up at the humans in the truck and snarling, showing off its large fangs.

Though Sammy had his head buried in Andrew's chest, Jake was as fascinated by the creature as his dad was. It meandered over to the stump they'd used as a table, and raised itself up on its hind legs. But that wasn't quite right. The creature was *standing* up on its hind legs like a person. That's when Jake noticed its front paws weren't exactly like dog's paws. Each was more like a hand with individual fingers ending in a sharp claw. This was confirmed a moment later when it opened up their little cooler, reached in, and removed a sandwich. It first attempted to chew right through the plastic baggie, then figured a way to get a claw inside and pull the food out. The other sandwiches quickly disappeared in the same manner.

"Dad, what're we gonna do now?" Jake whispered.

"I guess we wait a bit and see what it does," Andrew replied. "If it was going to attack us, it would've already. I think it's just lookin us over a bit."

Jake suddenly thought of an idea. "Dad," he whispered again, "can we call out on the cell phone? I think it's in the glove box."

Andrew's wife had bought them two of those emergency phones for Christmas. They kept one in each car in case of a breakdown.

"Okay, son, slowly and carefully, get it out. Let's not draw too much attention to ourselves."

Jake slithered his way down below the window and reached into the glove box. He pushed aside a few service papers, napkins, and the owner's manual and grabbed the cell phone. Quietly, he shut the little door and handed it over to his father.

Luckily, Andrew was able get a signal, even this far in the woods. However, being an emergency phone, the only number he could call was 9-1-1. As the other line began to ring, Andrew watched the creature finish up its investigation of their belongings on the stump and began walking *on two legs* toward the truck. It stood easily a foot or more taller than the truck cab, and its snarling maw was pulled back in what could only be described as a wicked grin. Andrew was so terrified he could barely speak into the phone.

***

Steve had watched the AML show whenever he could, and when he did get a chance to finally meet the wild and eccentric host Reggie Bushman, he was not disappointed. Towering several inches over the teacher, Reggie's high-heeled snakeskin boots and 10-gallon hat made him even more impressive. His barrel chest made the buttons on his bleached white, custom-leather shirt stretch to their limits. A red bandana was tied loosely around his deeply tanned neck. Reggie's long, handle-bar moustache completed the look of a biker crossed with a ranch hand. He was a fashion statement here in Twin Lakes, to be sure.

Unlike the crew that arrived midweek to avoid the traffic, Reggie had strategically planned his arrival for a Friday, right in the middle of the influx of tourists and weekend warriors. August 3, the Friday of the prime spotlight weekend of the summer. He wanted to make a scene, and he got it. The merchandise was out on display and selling like hotcakes. Reggie would spend many hours those first few days shaking hands, signing autographs, and promoting his wares. Thousands showed up on and off all weekend long just to be a part of the nationwide phenomena that is Hollywood.

Since Steve was only there as a liaison to the locals, and had essentially joined the ranks of the behind-the-scenes research crew, Reggie basically paid him little attention, other than the customary handshake. The big man had much more on his mind. Filming would commence shortly, and after the big promotional weekend, they only had a day to get their plans in order. Most of the afternoon and early evening that first day was spent under the big tent, the entire assembly of 17 crewmembers present.

Top priority was to locate and film at the locations of the sightings, then track down or bait the creature, tag it, and film it. Len Hayes' crew had filmed hours of second-unit shots, including all of the locations the research crew had dug up all over the state and the extensive work done in and around Twin

Lakes. The Crooked Creek State Forest gave them impressive shots. It was now time for Reggie to put it all together.

He had planned to begin filming lakeside with Sonny Chambers when an event, an actual sighting that moment, changed their plans immediately. They were about to have their first real encounter on Reggie's first day in town.

***

Deputies Van Pratt and Smitts pulled up to the AML tent and notified Reggie that they had a "hot one" out in the state forest. Normal departmental procedure would indicate that the police force should secure the scene and report back in to the chief before any media or other persons would be notified. But since the two young deputies were just itching to get themselves involved in the monster chase and potentially end up on camera on national television, a slight deviation was in order. Besides, the complaint they received didn't have any loss of life or limb attached to it, and honestly, it sounded just too good to pass up. This opportunity might not occur again.

Reggie and as many of the crew as could be spared then jumped into their trucks and Suburbans and tore off after the black-and-white squad car. They had only paused long enough to grab a few metal crates containing vital implements such as cameras and observation equipment. Luckily for the convoy, the impending night prevented any gawkers and fans from following them.

The fleet turned left at Twin Lake's only stoplight and proceeded over the interstate and east of town toward the state forest and the obscurity of approaching darkness. About a mile out of town, the squad car turned south onto the gravel of Marsh Road and entered the forest. The convoy of vehicles kept pace as the dirt road steadily narrowed until it became just a two-track, wide enough for one car at a time. Under the canopy of branches far overhead, all final remnants of daylight disappeared.

A few minutes later, the headlights of the police sedan shined brightly on the rear tailgate of an old pickup. The squad car pulled up next to the old Dodge, and the convoy of trucks and Suburbans fanned out, blasting their headlights out into the quiet and still forest all around. Car doors slowly creaked open and the men piled out, flashlights in hand, as they scanned the perimeter. An improvised film crew carried the smaller versions of the cameras and microphones they normally used for their shows, and Reggie Bushman primped himself before taking center stage.

The officers approached the old pickup and found Mr. Bierstone and his two sons alive and well, though quite shaken up after their encounter. The young deputies interviewed all three witnesses on camera, and were followed up by Reggie, who was much more eloquent and probing in his questioning. As soon as Andrew Bierstone indicated a direction the creature had come from and where it finally sauntered off to, crew members jumped into action, processing the scene and attempting to track the beast.

There was little to go on, since the creature had left the scene at least a half hour previously, but that didn't stop the *American Myths and Legends* crew. Reggie bought the possessions on the table stump, except for Sammy's toys and the car keys, for $200 cash, on the spot. There was no way Andrew could say no to that; he'd buy them all new woods jackets the next day, and have a wad of cash to spare. The crew hung around the scene for several hours, long after Andrew and his sons departed for home. The two deputies, enthralled in the energetic activity all around them, stuck around for as long as they could, until they were called back to the station to deal with a domestic dispute in town.

The little cooler was bagged for further inspection back at their mobile lab. Several hair samples were collected, and a number of plaster casts were made, though the tracks were so poor there wasn't much definitive about them. After a few hours with no sightings, the crew returned, packed up, and headed to the base camp to review all of the data.

All in all, it was an excellent start to this season's show. In fact, it was much more than Reggie expected on their first day of filming. Unlike a few of the other locations in previous years where the myth was more fictional than factual, there was real evidence here. This wasn't just a story passed along in the local bars. Something was prowling these woods. Something real had scared that man and his boys.

***

Unlike that exciting first day, the next two weeks were completely uneventful. There were no sightings and no encounters. Though the AML crew combed the state forest, no other evidence of the Dogman was found. It was as if the creature had just up and disappeared. Obviously a change of plans was in order. Reggie decided to draw in the creature with bait.

They chose a spot a bit to the west of the encounter with the wood-cutting family to set the trap. A pair of hunters in tree stands strategically placed around a bait pile that would tranquilize the creature. They set up so they were downwind of the meat. The remainder of the crew would be hunkered down tight until called upon. Each member used tiny earpieces and microphones so they could whisper to each other and not spook the prey. They set up in the early afternoon, and then settled down to wait patiently, all night and into the next day if necessary.

Their ammunition consisted of a specially handmade dart called a flechette. This was a hollow syringe filled with a tranquilizing drug in the shape of a long, narrow bullet. But unlike traditional bullets, the flechette's rear end flared out in several horizontal vanes for stability in flight. These were extremely lightweight, allowing the hunters to carry a number of rounds. They could be fired in semi-automatic weapons, so there was no wait to reload for a second shot. Reggie's special ammunition also included a bonus: each needle injected a microscopic GPS tracking computer chip that embedded itself under the target's skin. Even if the flechette was removed or knocked off the animal, the drug would be administered and the GPS chip would be implanted. Obviously, they wanted a clean shot and drop so they could scientifically measure and examine the body. But if something unusual happened, they could at least track it with the computers back at base camp.

The embedded GPS tracking chip was a vast improvement over the first design, which allowed the Bigfoot to escape a few years earlier. The initial model held the chip in the dart itself, which could be ripped out or scratched off on a tree or boulder. It had been perfected since. Reggie didn't want to be disappointed again.

Back in town, in the confines of the mobile command base, the tech crew, along with Chad, Markus, Tim, and Steve Nolan, waited patiently for the trap to spring. They were ready with the GPS tracking systems. Though they were out of harm's way, each man was just as nervous as those in the field.

Steve in particular was a nervous wreck. For months now, he was afraid of an inevitable connection with the creature. His dreams, so real, so unexplained, so horrific, forced him to explore the grim thought that *he* could be the creature. Was it so far-fetched, considering the nightmares he had? They seemed so much like actual memories. His own memories, though he couldn't recall any of them outside of his dreams. He didn't really believe in werewolves and such creatures, but when rational answers failed to give explanations, his mind turned to the irrational. If he and the creature were indeed somehow intimately connected, there'd be no sighting out in the woods this evening. He could only hope that something did show up there.

The crew put out half of the carcass of a cow to use as bait. Within hours, it had attracted all sorts of creatures from crows to a coyote. The crew waited. Reggie sat in one tree stand, his high-powered semi-automatic rifle resting on its tripod. Another tree stand was a hundred yards to his left, at a right angle to the bait pile. Between them they'd have an unobstructed view of the creature, and the one with the best shot would take it down.

They waited for several hours, and soon the sun was setting down below the tree line. Shadows slowly converged across the countryside. The hot air cooled, and became very still. No breeze blew across the leaves in the coming darkness.

"Tree one, this is tree two. Sir, I think I have a visual, 120 degrees, approaching from the east-southeast, about 400 yards away," reported the second tree stand. Everyone froze. No man in the crew wanted to be one who spooked the creature.

The report sounded through the speakers in the AML trailer back at base camp. Steve inhaled, holding his breath. This could be the moment of truth. If there was something out there, if the creature did emerge, it meant his irrational worries were for nothing. He waited, heart pounding in his chest, hands clenched in fists under the little work table.

Reggie very slowly raised his high-powered binoculars and turned his head without moving his torso. Yes, indeed, there was something big and black picking its way carefully through the woods toward the bait pile. A few seconds later the boss had his first glace at the Dogman. It was all the legends said, and more. It moved through the shadows so as to camouflage itself, its pitch-black stringy fur dangling from its lithe body. The Dogman was approaching on all fours, though every once in a while it stopped, stood on its hind legs, and raised its muzzle, sniffing the air. Its jaws were opened slightly, as it panted like a dog, and the long, sharp fangs curved in a menacing sneer. Once Reggie watched as it stood, reached out with one clawed hand, not a paw, and grasped a sapling, like a hiker would balance himself as he climbed over a downed tree. It was definitely a hand with individual fingers, all covered with the same midnight black fur. Its ears were tall and pointed straight upward. And indeed, the most striking aspect was the slanted, yellow eyes. They were set back in its head above the muzzle. And yes, like all the stories said, they were glowing with a supernatural light.

The Dogman was all Reggie had imagined and yet beyond all his expectations. Unlike some in his crew, Reggie totally and completely believed in the myths he uncovered. They never failed to fascinate him. Sometimes his search was in vain; other times there were clues and sightings. But never before had he been this close to the genuine article. This was a real creature, and not just a story or a myth.

Steve couldn't help but exhale in relief at the message from the field. Thank God! The others in the trailer looked over at him in surprise and annoyance. Steve was distracting them from their jobs, and from the best part of the narration. Unfortunately there were no cameras out to record the scene.

Reggie didn't want anything to possibly interfere with the shot and tagging of the creature. Far too many little things could spook the Dogman, and if it all worked out, they'd have plenty of opportunities to record all the video they wanted later on. But though there was no video, the audio came through loud and clear. Len Hayes very quietly narrated the incident unfolding in the woods for those crew members back in town. Embarrassed, Steve meekly apologized, and the other men returned their attention to the speakers whispering the events as they unfolded in the forest.

It was taking the bait. Everyone held his breath as the Dogman came across the carcass, but then looked around suspiciously. No one dared move. A few moments that seemed like hours went by, and then the creature bent over and began to feed. It tore out huge chunks of meat, barely chewing them before they disappeared down its gullet. It continued to feast, bloodying its claws and muzzle with the meat.

The report to the boss was barely audible: "Tree one, I have an obstruction. You'll have to take the shot."

Reggie leaned down and took aim through his scope. He'd practiced daily for years for this type of shot. He inhaled slightly as he pulled back on the trigger. The rifle gave a sharp crack, and a hundred yards away the creature rocked back, tumbling to the ground, as the dart slammed into its shoulder. Immediately, it jumped to its feet, roared with an intensity that caused everyone, even those back in the command trailer, to cover his ears against the searing pain, and bolted away from the carcass and on through the woods. Steve had never heard anything like it, not even on the worst monster movie ever made. It was a sound he hoped to never hear again.

"Okay, boys, let's start tracking it," the boss ordered. "The drug should begin taking effect immediately. It'll be crashed out cold in a minute."

The crew members started forward through the underbrush in the direction the creature had sprinted. They moved quickly, knowing the beast's adrenaline could push it a long way before it finally collapsed. Though the darkness hadn't fallen completely yet, each carried his own long-handled flashlight at the ready. The line of searchers extended out for over 200 feet, anywhere between 10 and 15 feet between each man. That would give them plenty of vision to look for signs and yet come to each other's aid if something wrong happened.

Immediately the crew back at the mobile lab in town began tracking the creature from its GPS signal. It was coming through crystal clear. But they were dismayed because the signal should have slowed down and eventually stopped due to the effects of the tranquilizer. However, the little blinking red dot on the computer screen kept up the dizzying pace away from the crew in the woods.

Though the team at ground zero kept searching through the night, they were unable to find much of a trace of the creature. They easily covered the ground where the beast should have fallen had the drug taken its intended effects.

"I don't understand it," growled an annoyed Reggie Bushman. "That tranquilizer would have dropped a horse in 30 seconds. "The creature should have just fallen over. I just don't get it." He'd pulled off his large Stetson hat and run his hands through his long, graying hair. He questioned the tech team back at headquarters. "Are you guys sure the GPS is still attached? It didn't come out, did it?"

"No, boss," came the reply. "It's still traveling at a high velocity away from your location. We're tracking it right now. I don't think you're going to see it again tonight."

Eventually, even the tracks disappeared, and so they reversed and covered back across the area they'd searched.

The tech crew back in town continued to track the creature through the GPS unit, and reported its flight far into the most remote areas of the state forest. There weren't even any roads back through there. They would continue to track it, changing shifts every few hours. However, it didn't make much sense for the team to remain in the forest. They might as well return and gather strength, planning for the ambush that would soon follow. The creature wasn't going anywhere as long as the GPS signal held up. They'd be able to find it at their leisure.

CHAPTER 10

September 2007

The CCC camp was one of the oldest civilized remains in the Twin Lakes area. Originally set up in the 1930s by the Roosevelt administration, the Civilian Conservation Corps brought the many unemployed young men from the cities out to rural America to complete all sorts of projects to improve facilities and rebuild the wilderness. Across the countryside, the CCC workers built roads, bridges, dams, and public buildings. They installed telephone and power lines. The urban work force also planted millions of trees, completed soil erosion prevention projects, and improved the stream beds. In the Twin Lakes area, the workers dredged the local rivers and constructed the sea walls, built up the logging trails into actual gravel roads, and put up the first schools and community buildings.

The Twin Lakes Area Camp was established in the north central section of the Crooked Creek State Forest, recently established by the joint effort of the National Parks Service and the Department of Agriculture. Over 105,000 acres makes it the largest state forest with a contiguous land mass. Less than a year after its designation, the state forest welcomed over 1,500 workers from Detroit, Flint, Saginaw, and other large cities in southern Michigan under the administration of the U.S. Army and leaders from the Department of Labor. Their first chore was to clear several acres to build the camp. Lumber from the massive trees was milled down on site and provided all the wood products the camp needed to get underway. Cement foundations were created for all of the cabin-like buildings, though the workers stayed in large army tents. By 1935, the camp was up and running smoothly, and the workers were gainfully employed in building projects in a six-county area.

The one thing the CCC administration didn't count on was the harsh northern Michigan winter. A year-round enterprise, the camp reacted in the best way it could to protect the lives of its civilian workers. They'd all freeze to death if they stayed out in the elements. So, they dug in. Literally. A massive and immediate plan was launched to build a network of basements under each cabin, connected by an elaborate series of tunnels and underground rooms. Some were fabricated with cement or brick, while others simply held back the soil with layers of wooden beams and planking. The cold, snowy weather enticed the workers to complete the task in record time, and within only a few weeks, everyone was bundled up in a fairly cozy retreat several feet beneath the blustery surface. Stone hearths were fabricated and chimneys vented up through the soil so fires could warm the rooms. Everyone hunkered down to wait out the winter.

Even today, the foundations of the old CCC camp can still be seen just to the north of Lookout Hill, that favorite stargazing spot. These foundations are all that is left to mark what was once a bustling little village in the north woods. The once proud cabins have since been returned to the natural elements, long after all of the workers returned south to their families. Most records of the camp had been lost to antiquity. Few people even knew it was ever there, and the cement foundations scattered over the former site were often a mystery to anyone who hiked through the area.

And the elaborate network of tunnels connecting the various foundation pieces? Many caved in naturally over the next 70 years. Some were used by vagrants and the homeless when necessary for shelter. Many became the homes of the various critters of the forest. Some were impassable. But for the most part, the underground maze of rooms and passageways still existed. It was dank, smelly, and extremely dirty. Some of the passages led to dead ends, blocked up by soil erosion. But a person, or animal, could still easily pass through most of the tunnels.

The camp's location in the very heart of the state forest, as well as its physical structure and design, made it a haven for anybody, or any thing, wishing to hide out. It was the perfect lair for the Dogman.

***

The GPS tracking unit was sending back excellent signals to the AML satellite relay truck. Reggie stood over the technician watching the small red blip on the screen. The modern technology they used displayed a highly detailed topographic map of the area being searched, in this case the Crooked Creek State Forest. And like many of the new online geosynchronous mapping systems, their maps could be zoomed in and out quickly and easily to pinpoint the tracking unit to within about 10 feet of its actual location. It was the best system money could buy, and it only came in a close second to the satellite tracking and mapping systems used by the U.S. armed forces.

"Switch over to thermal," Reggie ordered. Nick, the tech guy, complied, and the screen warped to black covered with myriad flowing, amorphous blobs of various colors. These were the heat signals given off by landforms, plants, and wildlife in the area. Cooler temperatures were in purple and blue, and warmer ones were yellow, orange, and red. The red dot changed to a red blur, displaying the body heat emanated by the creature. It was surrounded by a massive layout of deep purple and blue in what almost seemed to be a maze. "What is that place it's hiding?" the boss asked.

The tech started banging away on the keyboard. He pulled up all sorts of maps and information, but was unable to discern the strange, square and rectangular shapes or the weird paths between them. "From all I can tell, boss, it almost seems to be a little village, or it was once, though there's no mention of any buildings on any of my maps."

"Have you been tracking it constantly the past few days?" asked Reggie, staring intently at the map.

"Dave and I have taken turns on and off since the tracking unit went online. One of us has always been monitoring it."

"And what have we learned about its movements so far?"

"It has wandered off on various paths to the west, in the direction of town, right around sunset, and it's returned back to this location each morning. It has followed this pattern for the past three nights"

Reggie stood upright in deep thought, and rubbed his stubbled chin with the massive paw of his right hand. This is it, its lair. If ever there was a chance to capture the creature, it was there. Ideas poured through his mind. He'd be the first to actually detain a wild, legendary creature. Not only would this be the greatest moment of his career as a TV personality, but he could also corner the scientific arena, creating what could be the greatest biological discovery, possibly ever. Dollar signs began swimming with his thoughts.

"We'll need a plan to capture the beast, on camera," Reggie stated slowly and carefully. "It has to be set up at night when it's away. We'll spring the trap at dawn when it returns." The boss turned to one of his assistants. "Gather the troops. We'll have an emergency meeting in one hour under the big tent. I want this plan airtight and ready to put in action for tomorrow night!"

***

The two dark Suburbans crunched their way down the path toward the CCC camp, then came to a halt at a sandy turnaround. Then men climbed out quietly, ignoring the *No Trespassing* signs, and carefully trying not to disturb the natural environment much. They were dressed in black with night vision goggles and small headsets consisting of an earpiece and tiny microphone wire. They could easily talk to each other in low tones and still hear the information sent to them by Nick, the lab tech, back at base camp in town. Dave, the other tech, had accompanied the covert operations crew now assembling their wares in the forest. The only ones back in the satellite communications trailer at the village green were Nick, Markus, Tim, Chad, and Steve. The five of them huddled around the various video screens and the GPS tracking unit. The red dot was several miles away, doing its own thing, apparently wandering through the woods. There would be plenty of time to set the trap.

Reggie's crew took their jobs as seriously as any paramilitary organization could. Miniature remote cameras were hooked in trees all around the site, along with ultra-sensitive microphones. Guy wires and snares were set up in strategic locations. And Len Hayes was out there filming the entire operation for posterity. Within an hour, the trap was set. They had only to wait for their quarry.

Under the full cover of night, the men gathered in a group around a set of cement slab foundations. Their night vision enabled them to see down into the holes and cave-ins and make an evaluation of the network of tunnels and caverns.

"What is this place?" asked one crew member. "It's like some underground hideout gone wild. If it weren't so far in the middle of nowhere, my kids would love playing in it."

Reggie puffed out his chest. "I'm going down there to see. Anybody coming with me?" His sidearm, a huge 45-caliber cannon of a handgun, strapped to his right thigh, the big man carefully climbed down the eroded embankment, followed by two others. They inspected the immediate area thoroughly, and then began creeping down a tunnel. Reggie was far too big for the passageway, so he had to duck and bend his knees just to keep moving forward. They kept in contact with the men above, narrating their every find.

"There are some really old signs of human habitation here." Reggie held up an old tin drinking cup. "This place must have had some significance somewhere back in history."

"Boss, look here," commented one of the men poking down a side tunnel where it opened up into a large, underground room. The other two followed him inside. A foul stench greeted each at the doorway. They all turned their heads away, necks straining and noses wrinkling up. The chamber was littered with bones of all sorts, scattered all around. Most were little, obviously the remains of critters and small animals. But there was a carcass of what could only be a deer or elk, half eaten in the corner. The heavy aroma of the rotted flesh nearly made the three men throw up. This was it, the creature's lair.

Back at the base camp, Nick and the USC boys were adjusting the bank of small monitors up at eye level. Each one was tuned into a different remote camera mounted on a tree at the trap site. While they tinkered, Steve had kicked back, relaxing finally, and stared off absently at the GPS screen, and the little red blinking dot. All of this elaborate setup just to nab that red spot, he thought. He continued to stare at it while the others continued their preparations. It *was* searching for something, Steve suddenly thought. That creature had been systematically working its way closer and closer to town, investigating every shack, cabin, and person along the way. He thought back to his strange dreams, running through the forest, dead certain he was searching for something. Absently, he fiddled with the gemstone around his neck. Every 10 years the creature reappeared. Those same years his sleep was interrupted by the strange and awful dreams. Was there a connection? Was he somehow connected to it?

The blinking red dot caught his attention again. How long had it been in that same spot, he wondered? He gazed at it a while longer. It wasn't moving. Maybe it had found something to feed upon. Or maybe...

"Nick, how could you know if the GPS track had somehow fallen off?" Steve asked, sitting upright in his little swivel chair.

"Well," Nick paused, thinking for a second. "When the unit smashed in California a few years ago, the tracking dot just stopped. The computer chip was okay, but it obviously wasn't moving with the creature anymore. This new chip is set under the skin with the flechette. It shouldn't come off, theoretically."

"Theoretically, might it look anything like this?" Steve asked in a worried tone. He pointed to the computer screen, the red dot blinking innocently, but not moving one millimeter.

"Oh, my God," Nick stammered. The others had crowded around as the tech sat down at the console. "How long's it been stationary like this?"

"I just noticed it, but I've been staring at it for minutes now and don't recall it moving at all," replied Steve.

Nick hurriedly put his earpiece and microphone on, contacting the crew in the woods. "Reggie, you guys gotta get outta there, right now! We've lost the GPS track, I repeat, we've lost the GPS unit. We can't see where the creature is!"

Reggie's voice came in, with just a hint of static, over the earpieces. "What do you mean you lost it? Get the signal back."

"It's just like a few years ago. I think the GPS unit has been separated from the creature. I have no idea where the thing is." Nick was doing his best to keep from panicking, but it obviously showed in his voice.

Reggie refused to panic. "Go to the infrared and scan the area. You should be able to see something. It'll have a larger heat index than most things around here."

Nick keyed in a few commands, and his monitor switched over to the colorful display, now mostly the deep hues of black, blue, and violet because of the night. The initial scan showed thousands of tiny heat spots, but as they zoomed into the area, there were fewer to watch. Unfortunately, there was one larger, fuzzy red blur moving rapidly across the screen. Everyone in the tech trailer stared alarmingly at the computer image, barely able to comprehend the speed at which the red blip was returning toward the crew's location.

"Sir, we've reacquired the creature," Nick said slowly. "It's on its way back to you. Estimated time of arrival is..." He paused to do a little mental math. "ETA is less than two minutes. You've gotta get outta there, sir!"

Reggie quietly whispered, "We won't have time without alerting the creature. If it hears us, the trap is ruined. This is the only shot we've got. We're going to capture it right now."

The boss turned to his companions in the passageway. "Boys, we're down here for the duration. The rest of you slip down here too; you'll never make it back to the Suburbans. The trap's set above us, we'll be fine here underground. I want all of us to go silent. Nick, you'll have to be our eyes and ears."

The rest of the crew quickly dropped down into the system of tunnels and padded down the passageway. The men hunkered down, steeling themselves for whatever came next. This would be the first opportunity for most of them to see the Dogman for themselves. Some were excited, dying to see a real myth come to life. Others would certainly have been elsewhere if at all possible.

It was dead silent down in the catacombs. The men barely breathed. Nick continued to count down the distance between the creature and their location. "One thousand yards...five hundred yards...two hundred yards...one hundred yards...Sir, it's right on top of you."

Reggie unlatched the strap of his holster, and silently pulled out his sidearm. He'd affectionately named it 'Thunder' because of blast it made when it was fired. The rest of the crew quietly and quickly backed behind their boss. If (or when) he started shooting, they didn't want to be in the way. Other than Reggie, the field crew was armed only with small hand knives and long flashlights on each person; their firearms were still stowed neatly in the vehicles.

Steve and the crew back in town were eternally thankful they'd stayed behind that night.

The little cameras were intended to shoot film in daylight or in complete darkness if necessary. It wouldn't have mattered anyway, because the entire clash took place in the tunnels and rooms below the ancient CCC camp. However, the microphones worked fine, and sent back plenty of gruesome sounds and noises. No one back in town saw the dark shadow slip past the cameras and drop down into the catacombs. But they did hear the low growl echo through the speakers in the tech trailer, followed soon after by the thunderous boom of Reggie's hand gun. Screams and cries for help were quickly silenced behind the roaring of both the creature and the collapsing foundation that echoed through the underground tunnels. The men didn't stand a chance; the skirmish was over in a matter of seconds as the crew was buried beneath tons of cement, rock, and earth. The last sound transmitted was the triumphant howling of the creature before it evacuated the area.

Some in the tech crew stared open-mouthed at the computer screen in disbelief. Not a soul made a sound. Tim sat down on the swivel chair with his head buried in his hands, streams of tears sliding down his cheeks. Steve could barely believe it. They were all gone in the blink of an eye. He fingered the little gemstone on his necklace again.

Though the AML crew had set out to capture the legendary beast on film, all they had really done was to aggravate the creature.

***

A day later, Steve sadly said goodbye to the four remaining members of the once proud team. A fun time and an exciting ride had ended with tragic finality. The shocked faces told it all, even days afterward. Of course the show would be canceled, their footage and data confiscated by the parent company that owned AML. Somewhere the lawyers and insurance companies were gearing up for their own battles to settle everything legally. A mass of people, especially celebrities, couldn't just die without someone being blamed or sued.

The USC boys piled into one of the trucks, and headed down the highway. The cable company had sent in a cleanup crew to pack up the gear and return the trailer and vehicles to headquarters in San Jose. It was the swift, bitter end to a Hollywood era.

No one in town knew exactly what happened out in the state forest, except for Steve and the local officers who had to identify the various remains. But there were plenty of rumors and speculation. Some even thought the AML guys got what they deserved. Those *No Trespassing* signs were there for a reason. Hell, the men were far more destructive and deadly to themselves than that 'supposed' creature was. The base camp in town was dismantled, cleaned up, and moved in the quiet of a Sunday morning. Only a handful of residents even saw them leave.

Steve's only memento from the entire affair was the little, worn journal Markus gave him before he left. It was the same diary the researcher had received from the old Indian a few months earlier. His spirits depressed, Steve was reluctant to open the little book, and instead tossed it on his coffee table. He'd read it, he promised himself. Eventually. Just not right now. The school year had started up again, and Steve was more than swamped getting his classes underway. To his disappointment, his free time wasn't taken up by the AML crew any more. They'd provided a much needed distraction from the doldrums of every day school life.

***

Steve's dreams changed dramatically after the AML disaster. No longer did he envision the intruder on the mound. These were replaced by far more violent episodes. Still he felt the connection to the beast; he was the creature in the dreams.

The feelings and emotions he felt in his sleep rose to an anger focused not on retrieving the missing item but on protecting his territory. The dreams were becoming epics lasting all night, each a great deluge that forcefully carried him along to the inevitable end; he couldn't wake himself to interrupt the nightmare even if he wanted to.

Though he wasn't anywhere near the brutal scene when it happened, he could see it all so clearly: the earthen tunnels, the chipped concrete, the dirty roots poking through the walls and ceilings. He (the creature) stalked the prey to his (its) lair, but when he (it) rounded the final corner, the shooting began. The big man pulled the trigger once, twice, three times. The thunder echoed through the tight passageway. All the shots missed their intended target, but instead blew out two feet of the rotted support beam in the doorway. Steve (the creature) jumped back and sprinted for the exit as a chain reaction began, the doorway crumbling, followed by its overhead beam, and then the ceiling beams in the room occupied by the men. The entire catacomb was filled by the bulk of the rocks, earth, and cement slab foundations several feet above. There was no way the men could get out. Steve (the creature) listened to the men desperately attempting to escape, or struggling for their last breath as tons of weight crushed the life from them.

An ominous thought passed through his mind at the conclusion of the dream. The creature was becoming more feverous in its search for whatever it was looking for. It would abandon its now demolished lair in the wilderness and move on to more populated areas. It was now angry that men had invaded its den. It would have no leniency on any humans it encountered from this point forth.

Steve awoke the morning after that first new dream, shaking and breathless as usual, absolutely sure that the creature was soon to become far more aggressive and dangerous than it had been all year. His connection to the creature was still unclear to him, even though the clues he so desperately needed to convince himself were written down in an old little journal in his living room.

***

At six-foot-three and 225 pounds, Doug Martin was a major college prospect at quarterback. He'd led his team to the state semi-finals in 2006, and they were currently undefeated after six weeks this season. Doug had the all-American looks to match his physique. A typical week saw him turn down several potential dates so he could concentrate on his sport. It wasn't that he disliked girls at all; it's just that most wanted relationships and all. They wanted to hang on the arm of the handsome and popular quarterback, but his priorities were in other areas.

Mr. Martin was already counting up the millions his son would earn in his future NFL contract. It didn't matter that Doug Sr. was already pulling in six figures from a leading auto company in Detroit. He had the fever so many fathers (and mothers too) get by living through his son. He was sure his son would be the next superstar.

But Doug really didn't like all the hype, the craziness of football. All week long was spent preparing and practicing, and Friday nights were just wild. Sure, he enjoyed playing. He was good at it, and he was a natural leader. For him, the best part of the games was the competition itself: matching up his skill, leading his troops against the opponents. In his playing years, his teams were generally so superior to their opponents that there wasn't much of a game. Doug relished the games against truly excellent rivals. Even if his team lost, he could take pride in the knowledge he played his best, he gave it his all. He believed the true glory in sports wasn't winning games; it was in competing against far better adversaries, even if losing in the process.

He could do without the periphery surrounding the games. He nearly loathed the fanfare, the cheering crowds, and the endless journalists. So many people had such high expectations for him; sometimes he just hated it all.

But he didn't share his father's excitement about playing football in college. In many ways, he felt trapped. Sure he was good at his sport, and he knew he'd need a college education to get a decent job. He couldn't work in the auto industry like so many in the past. There was no way he would be an executive like his father. He often thought about being a football coach, since he knew the game so well and was truly good at the strategy and leadership. The way he looked at the whole situation, an athletic scholarship would get him into a good university at least. Otherwise, his mediocre grades alone might allow him to attend a community college. He could keep playing for several more years if it paid for his schooling.

What he'd really like to do, if he had his choice, was to move up permanently to Twin Lakes. He'd wake up early every morning and fish as the sun came up, and then spend his days either relaxing on the water or hiking or mountain biking through the woods. He was an outdoorsman at heart, regardless of living in the city for 10 months of the year. Doug cherished the weeks in the summer when he and his family moved up north into their cottage. Actually, it was bigger than the homes of most of the year-round residents, with 150 feet of frontage on Long Lake, a huge boathouse with a bow rider and two jet skis, and a large deck complete with hot tub and plenty of outdoor furniture for entertaining dozens of people.

Five bedrooms and a bunk house over the garage enabled large groups to congregate in the cottage at any time, and often his parents' friends spent long weekends in the little paradise.

He loved to just escape it all, head off into the woods, and lose himself in the endless trails for hours. Doug knew them all well, having walked and biked them for years. It was a 15-minute ride down the back roads from his house on Long Lake to the state forest. Once there, Doug could bike for hours, putting all thoughts of football and his future out of his mind. Getting lost was a joke. He'd just find his way home when he was ready.

Two weeks after the AML debacle, on the last Saturday of September, Doug rode off into the state forest. Because of football season, he hadn't been up north since the end of July, and had of course failed to hear of the wild events occurring in the woods outside town. Even if he had heard the stories, they wouldn't have stopped him. He was young, fearless and indestructible. In his mind, he'd live forever. So too were such thoughts of invulnerability coursing through many young people just before something awful happens to them.

***

When Doug didn't show up for dinner, his parents were mildly annoyed. He had a penchant for disrupting their precious time schedules. But they weren't worried until an hour after dark. They started making calls to everyone they knew, from friends and neighbors and finally to the Twin Lakes police department. Deputy Van Pratt, on duty for the evening, assured the parents that Doug was probably fine; maybe he'd met up with a local girlfriend. Anyway, he wasn't officially "missing" until 24 hours passed. But the deputy told them he'd make a call to the officers and the county sheriff's office and they'd see if anything unusual had arisen. By morning, Mrs. Martin was hysterical. Douglas was pissed off because, though he might be a bigwig downstate, he had little influence over the local police up here.

At 7:00 AM, Mr. Martin met the chief at the door to the police office. The chief had barely gotten Douglas to stop swearing and following him into the office when the chilling call came over the scanner. A pair of joggers out hitting the trails at dawn had uncovered a mangled mountain bike covered with what appeared to be blood. Further investigation by Deputy Smitts, who was the first on the scene, led to the discovery of the body of a teenaged Caucasian male floating face down in the waters of Crooked Creek. Though he wasn't an expert on dead bodies, Smitts knew this one had been dead for several hours at least. Mr. Martin was in shock as the chief took down the location, calmly called the county coroner and several other deputies, and escorted him to the chief's cruiser.

A silent ride ended 10 minutes later as the chief's sedan reached the scene. Already deputies had cordoned off the area. Mr. Martin jumped out of the cruiser even before it rumbled to a stop, and the deputies were no match for him as he pushed his way to the creek. The officers watched as he stopped, looked down, and then pulled his fingers through his wispy hair. "Noooooo!" shrieked the old man as he fell to his knees at the top bank of the creek, shaking uncontrollably. "Noooo!" His shriek rose to a howl of rage and anger intertwined with grief. "No, no, no, no, nooo!"

After a few minutes of crying into his hands, Mr. Martin was led back to the cruiser by a pair of deputies as the coroner, who had just shown up, took charge of the scene. The chief was glad someone else could take charge of this mess. He'd secure the area and allow the coroner to boss around the deputies who were gathering evidence.

The crime scene immediately around the creek and body was a scuffled mess. The soft ground and mud around the creek held three distinct impressions, those of the mountain bike, Doug's cross-trainers, and the tracks of a large animal. There was no mistaking the size of the tracks, nor the claw marks at the top edge of each. They were distinctly those of a large predator, and they looked like the prints of a canine, though they were four or five times larger than any dog, coyote, or wolf tracks the deputies had ever seen. And they were oddly elongated. With a little imagination, which didn't take much after all the year's incidents, they looked far too human as well. The body and the ground all around were covered with the long, coarse hairs of some animal, probably the one that created the tracks and apparently tousled with the boy. There were cuts and bruises on the body as well as gashes and rips on the clothing.

The deputies attributed the entire incident to the Dogman. What else could have done this? Considering the mess out at the CCC camp, it was the logical decision. Chief Thompson was getting quite aggravated by the mere mention of the creature, but he finally had to admit to himself that there was something out there, and it was damned dangerous. This was a new one to him; not in all his years of law enforcement did he ever have to deal with a wild creature outright attacking and killing people. And he couldn't think of anyone else he knew or had ever read of having to deal with such a situation. It was the substance of bad horror movies, not real life. But here he was, stuck right in the middle of a nightmare come alive.

The coroner's report later that afternoon stated the cause of death was by drowning. The body did have several lacerations on the arms, wrists, and hands, indicating there was some sort of struggle. And there was a blunt-force impact to the side of the head, just behind the right ear. Something (or someone) had struck Doug with enough force to knock him out and send him sprawling into the creek where his lungs filled with water.

The word spread through town like wildfire. Many locals knew young Doug, by sight at least, since he was always polite and respectful, and always out in public. It didn't take long for them to hear of the evidence that was collected, and the opinions of the young deputies. Immediately the blame was pushed on the Dogman. The creature went from being a scary legend that was fairly unbelievable to a real, serious threat in the span of minutes. Some even blamed the AML crew for either bringing the problem down on them in the first place or stirring up something that was now out of control. The town enacted a curfew, parents stopped allowing their kids outside to play, and many of the residents talked quietly about finding ways to eradicate this animal problem.

What many didn't realize was that they were about to get their chance to bite back.

CHAPTER 11

October 2007

The $50,000 reward for the carcass of the creature was placed by Mr. Martin in major newspapers all across Michigan and in several neighboring states. Little attention was paid to its timing; it was simply placed out of grief and anger, and vengeance. Mrs. Martin was doped up on valium, and Mr. Martin was going to use every penny he had if necessary to find and destroy the beast that killed his only son. However, this one family's dedication to retaliation would quickly cost even more lives in the town they loved.

Every rental cabin and hotel room for 25 miles around was completely booked up within 24 hours of the news hitting the media. Those who couldn't find a room slept in their campers, trucks, SUVs, and even cars. The interstate off-ramp was a constant procession of vehicles for nearly two days. The local businesses loved it. To make up for the previous poor winter and the high gas prices that kept many tourists away during the summer, they weren't about to deny the early-season hunters anything they wanted. This was the opportunity of a lifetime, besides the chance to fully recover from the winter slump and less-than-average summer. When else would the town ever be packed in the middle of October again? Regardless of the reason, there were consumers here in massive numbers, and the locals were happy to oblige.

Every business in town was booming. Lines formed at the fast food and sit-down restaurants. Party stores were hopping. Sales of ammunition, hunting and camping supplies, and gasoline were far surpassed by food and beer. Usually the beer trucks made a delivery once each week from October through April, but the local distributor wasn't going to miss out either. The trucks unloaded their wares every other day for three straight weeks.

Most of the so-called hunters would never even make the state forest. Too many would be drunk and passed out in hotel rooms, cabins, or in makeshift hunting camps. Still another large percentage would actually head into the woods but make so much noise that everything for miles around was scared off. This was the real danger: so many people in the woods in so close of an area, many well within range of several others. All it would take to set off World War III was a few shots in a crowded acre of woods.

The big reward was bringing up the novices and non-hunters as well as those seasoned in the sport. Anybody who thought he could look through a sight and pull a trigger wanted a shot at the money. There were plenty of car-loads who'd even vowed to share the reward, and they figured there'd be strength (and success) in numbers.

Of course, the local law enforcement agencies were overwhelmed. Though the part-time summer help was normally let go at the end of September, the chief had no choice but to keep them on. The township held an emergency meeting and immediately voted to spend the AML money to keep the four part-time officers fully employed to deal with the situation. The chief shared his department's concerns with the township supervisor and committee. The situation was nearing a disastrous level, he told them over and over. But he was outvoted by the committee of local businessmen and women, very willing to overlook a few "energetic and enthusiastic" sportsmen who were boosting the area's economy. The chief was instructed to keep order but not stop the hunters from spending their money in town.

Most of the town council still didn't believe in the whole thing anyway, and they felt the hunters would just wander around the woods like idiots looking for something that didn't even exist. The local businesses would still get the cash influx.

But even with the full staff normally reserved for the busy summer months, the chief's office was still swamped. At 6:50 AM on October 8th, the chief sauntered his way into the cramped police headquarters as he did every weekday morning and poured himself a cup of coffee. Gary Mcade, his second in command, was there waiting for him, exasperated. That was strange, since his shift technically didn't even begin until 7 AM. He'd been there for some time already. After sitting down in his old swivel chair, and taking a sip of the strong brew, the chief looked up at the deputy and said, "Okay, give me the bad news."

"Chief, there's no way we can keep up with all these hunters," Gary said wearily. "Four days now, and they're everywhere. So far they're not doing anything illegal. A few drunk 'n' disorderlies, that's all. So far it's even okay to go out and sight their rifles. Technically, we can't get them for hunting unless they shoot something. But it's obvious why they're here. I mean, this is way worse than opening day. We've got the real hunters out trying to bow hunt, and then all these morons show up expecting to use guns."

"You don't really think there's actually anybody out there with a bow instead of a firearm, do you?"

The town was always abuzz on November 15, Michigan's opening day of rifle season. The local buck pole often welcomed hundreds of hunters and even a bad year would see 80 deer hanging by the time awards were given out. For each hunter who bagged a deer during the 15-day season, there were 10 out in the woods who missed out. But the sheer numbers of hunters in the community right now just dwarfed the best the area would ever see.

Even bow season, which started on October 1, always brought up plenty of hunters. But this year, odds were good everyone in the woods would be carrying a rifle of some sort.

"Either way, the whole state forest is saturated with hunters," the deputy replied. "It's gettin' dangerous out there."

"Well, can't you get the guys out there and stop some of them? At least slow 'em down?" the chief asked, exasperated.

"Chief, even if we could get out on the back trails where they're hiding and find these guys, and let's say we did arrest some for reckless endangerment, we'd be spending all day transporting 'em back here where we certainly don't have room to house more than a dozen. You know that. We could fill up the county and state lockups and still not make a dent in that crowd."

"What did County say?" The chief already had a good guess. Twin Lakes was just a little town 20 miles from the much larger county seat of Cheboygan. Folks up there often tried to forget the rest of the county existed, except when it was tax time.

"They're going to assign three of their cars to the southern end of the county, that's it. But mostly they're just laughing at us. They don't buy any of this fiasco. It's our problem, not theirs, and they really couldn't care less."

"Have you called the DNR in on this? At least they could be out writing tickets."

"They're already out in full force, but with bow season already under way, they're way too overextended. They can't bring in anybody to help from around the state 'cause they're covering the hunting in their own counties."

"And what's the latest word from the state police?"

"They called last night and said the governor is denying your request to bring in the National Guard. She doesn't believe in this monster myth any more than I do, and she refuses to give it any legitimacy. They'll cover the expressway, and that's it. We're pretty much on our own."

"How about our locals? Can you at least get them out of the woods?"

"Chief, have you had a chance to check out the cars in town? They're from all over—Ohio, Indiana, Wisconsin—and I even wrote a ticket to a guy from Tennessee yesterday. He said he heard about the reward on the radio out of Knoxville. A few hours up I-75 and his SUV's here, and loaded for bear, let me tell you. I think most of our locals are smart enough to stay at home and avoid this whole mess."

"Yeah, that's wishful thinking," the chief said sarcastically. "You know as well as I do that there are plenty of folks up here who'd hunt all night long if they had a real shot at $50,000. To them, it's a better shot than they'd have winning the lottery."

"So, what are your orders?"

"Keep in constant contact with the DNR, and get everyone out in the back roads all day. That's where any action's going to be. Make sure you're all writing tickets, as many as you can, all day long. If we can't stop the rising tide, we might as well line the pockets of the township too."

"What're you going to do?"

"I'm staying in town and holding down the fort. I'm too old to be chasing any souls through the woods, real or imagined."

***

The chief had his suspicions about the so-called hunters out in his woods. But if he really knew what some of those people brought up north with them, he'd probably have a coronary. Simple and archaic means were all over the place: old rusty bear traps, snares, and all sorts of knives, hatchets, and axes. Rifles, pistols, and shotguns were very popular. And then there were the exotic ones, including crossbows, laser-sighted guns, and automatic weapons. There were even a few who brought dynamite and even worse things with them. Certainly all the ingredients for disaster were being handled by amateurs who'd been consuming far too much booze. And their minds were battling the effects of alcohol with thoughts of a large cash payday.

Stories at the local bars each night revolved around what various hunters had seen, shot, and missed by just hairs. At least once every few hours some fool would wander in and stammer that he'd seen some dark canine-shaped shadow, and all would hush around him. But within a few moments they realized the newcomer was full of crap and go back to their partying. Yes, there were a few kills. Several bears and coyotes were shot, along with countless deer and even a few elk. Most of the venison was quickly taken back to camp (or home) and cleaned and cooked before the DNR could catch the poachers. But in terms of the reward, truth was, no one saw anything close to the creature's description.

That is, until October 16th.

***

The small makeshift hunting camp was quiet as all six men were out scouring the woods of the state forest. Not one of them had any significant experience in hunting, or in tracking for that matter. Each had fired his rifle on practice ranges outside Columbus, Ohio, and though several did travel up to Michigan to hunt each fall, only one had ever actually bagged a deer (and that was four years ago), and it was a small doe at that. Mostly they went to hunting camp to escape their wives, families, and job obligations for a few days and just enjoy living the "manly" life out in the wilderness, and the opportunity to actually kill a deer was truly an afterthought. Of course, to hear them talk about their trips, you'd think they were big time hunters.

Duffy Morgan was the ringleader of the group. Tall and broad-shouldered, his physical size served him well as a factory foreman back home. He didn't take any gruff from anybody. His grandparents once owned a rustic, log-sided lakeside cabin he would visit every summer of his first 16 years. He was very familiar with the Twin Lakes area, and even after the old cabin was sold, Duffy still traveled north for another 30-some-odd years to vacation and hunt.

Jeff Brewster married Duffy's younger sister 20 years ago, and the two men had since been inseparable. They even lived down the street from each other. Both were experts on the gas grill, and family cookouts were culinary events every Sunday. Jeff was a stark contrast to his brother-in-law. Skinny though muscular, he still had a thick shag of hair while Duffy had been balding since the early 1990s. Jeff was quite laid-back while Duffy was uptight, always needing to be in charge.

The other four hunting companions worked under Duffy in Columbus. Mark Simmons, Ed Mustafa, Mike Harting, and Jack Delacroix joined Duffy and Jeff in a local summer softball league, and the six men played poker and drank a lot of beer together at least once a week all year long.

In reality, they were legends in their own minds. But here they were, tramping through the majestic north woods, joining thousands of others from all over the Midwest, the great white hunters aiming to find and kill a wild animal for a $50,000 reward. The way the men from Columbus figured it, they had just as much of a chance as anybody else.

What they didn't know was they were way in over their heads.

The mass of hunters might actually have had a chance in finding and shooting the creature they sought if they, as a whole, could sit still and wait in normal hunting blinds. But the hundreds of men with little or no hunting experience absolutely ruined their chances. Some constantly fired their weapons, either in sighting practice (being bored) or more commonly at shadows and noises their over-keen minds mistook for their quarry. Others wandered through the woods, snapping twigs, rustling leaves, and generally making all sorts of racket that would scare up every living thing for miles around.

An overhead view of the forest would have shown far too many men saturating a far too small space. All were trigger-happy, wanting a piece of that reward money. Far too many were challenged by an overabundance of alcohol or a lack of sleep or both. And of course, no one knew exactly what they were hunting. They only knew some type of large animal, a predator of some sort, needed extermination. It was a dangerous situation, to say the least.

The day was overcast, the sky a soup of dark gray clouds blended with white, and all stretching and reforming as the cold wind slid them quickly overhead. Each hunter with at least half a brain was bundled up tightly, wool jackets, car harts, and thick boots donned by most.

Just after a dinner of fried potatoes and steaks, and of course a few beers each to wash it all down, the Columbus group was loaded and ready for action. They had been staking out an area of around 50 acres of low swampland laden with scrubby pines and birch trees for the past few days, but had seen nothing. This was their last night here at camp, their last chance at the reward money, and they were itching for something to shoot at.

Dusk came on quickly because of the dark clouds, casting shadows through the swampy woods. To add to the gloom, a light ground fog began developing, hiding the lower trunks of the pines. Good visibility dropped to a matter of yards as the twilight spread over the forest.

Duffy was the first to see the dark shape moving through the brush off to his right. He was resting on a downed log a few yards up the side of the rise of land at the edge of the swamp. He was yawning in a grand fashion, nearly nodding off in spite of himself. The big dinner and cold beverages were taking their toll on him. After several days of seeing nothing, he had to blink his eyes, then rub them, then shake his head slightly to make sure he wasn't imagining it. His tiredness was forgotten immediately. Though the visibility wasn't the best, the dark shape was definitely an animal, as it was prowling forward on all fours. But even in the dim light, he could tell this wasn't a normal inhabitant of the Michigan woods. He'd hunted here for years, and knew all of the creatures up north. This one didn't belong here. He wasn't sure it belonged anywhere. It appeared to be wolf-like in stature, but it was so much more. The fur was thick, midnight black, and stringy. Its legs seemed too slender to support the massive chest. But even in the darkness, he could see all four legs were powerful and sinewy, surefooted on any terrain. As the creature passed between the black and white birch trees, Duffy guessed it stood at least four feet at the shoulder, far bigger than any wolf he'd ever heard of.

All thoughts of his companions were lost as he slowly and silently stood and raised his rifle. A moment later the creature stepped into an opening in the brush. It was a perfect shot, 20 yards away. Duffy tucked the butt of the rifle into his shoulder, raised the barrel, took aim through the sight, and inhaled, ready to pull the trigger. At that instant the creature turned its head and looked straight at him, slanted eyes glowing yellow in the darkness. Duffy hesitated, and it cost him. The creature leapt forward and away from the hunter, who recovered and fired, though the shot went just wide.

Duffy strode forward, attempting a second shot when the creature stopped, looked back at him, and then stood up on its hind legs. That just isn't right, he thought to himself, dropping the barrel of the rifle a bit. Animals don't stand up like a person. The powerful legs seemed just as natural holding it upright as they did bounding on all fours. It turned up its lips to reveal long, sharp fangs as its eyes narrowed, training on the human. A deep howl emerged from its maw, chilling the hunter to the bone. Duffy didn't wait another second. He raised the rifle up and pulled the trigger again, and this time his shot was true, the bullet slamming into its left shoulder and rocking it backward several feet. The creature hit the ground, rolled over its right shoulder and landed on all fours facing the hunter. It shook itself slightly, rolling the injured shoulder in a far too human fashion, like a weightlifter shrugging unconcernedly, and gazed again malevolently at Duffy, who couldn't believe this beast was still coming for him. He still had a great shot, and pulled the trigger again. Click. The rifle misfired. Duffy looked down at the rifle, and that was the moment the creature needed to change from defense to attack. Duffy looked up in time to see the beast coil its legs under for a spring. He was close enough that it could be on him in two leaps.

But before the creature could attack, it suddenly was knocked off balance, slamming into a tall birch a yard to its right. Just afterward came the crack of the rifle shot, catching up to the bullet. One of his companions had just saved his life. The creature staggered to its feet, on all fours again, howled in pain and confusion, and bounded off into the mist as Jeff came jogging up, out of breath from the short sprint. The two didn't have to speak, they just nodded to each other in complete understanding. Duffy reloaded his rifle quickly.

Another shot rang out off to their left, followed by a horrible, inhuman howl that echoed through the fading daylight. Another shot, and a few seconds later a far too-human scream of agony. Both recognized the voice as Mark's. Without thinking of safety, the two strode forward quickly and purposefully, rifles held up at the ready, toward the continuing screams. Another blast split the air, and the two hunters broke into a brisk trot, barely careful enough to avoid the downed logs and muddy soil. Within a minute, they found Mark rolling on the soft ground covered in dirt and blood. He'd been shot in the upper right chest, and was bleeding quickly. The two men were lucky they had kneeled down to check on their friend as a bullet flew directly overhead.

"Hey, we're right here," hollered Duffy into the darkness. "Stop shooting this way!"

A voice, probably Jack's, replied, "Okay, we're coming over. Stay where you are."

Jeff had removed his flannel jacket and torn off part of his own shirt to patch the gaping hole in Mark's back. He did his best to use pressure from his right hand to at least slow the bleeding, while his left hand gripped Mark's tightly. "Hang on, man, just stay with me," he told his friend. "We're gonna get you outta here."

A dark shape appeared through the mist, and Duffy momentarily mistook it for one of his companions. That is, until the glowing yellow eyes emerged from the apparition's visage. Duffy raised his rifle and began shooting wildly in the creature's direction. It jumped one way, then the next as the bullets screamed past it. Another human shriek pierced the twilight. That's when the carnage began.

Shots rang out all around the swamp. Unfortunately, all of the hunters had heard Duffy and Jack's voices and had converged on their companions. As they grew nearer, each saw the dark shape of the beast as it bolted first in one direction, then another in the gloom. Duffy's mad shooting launched them all into a frenzy, each firing at the dark shadow as it came into view. Cries and screams of fury, pain, and agony filled the woods. After what seemed like minutes of firing, but was actually only a matter of seconds, the shots ended abruptly. Only low groans and mutterings could be heard in the darkness.

***

Steve's dream took on a new perspective this evening. He was looking down from a bird's eye view on a forest floor. Even though he knew it was dark, and there was a bit of fog on the ground, he could see every object with great clarity. Six men lay prone and unmoving, covered with blood, sweat, and dirt. All were within 30 feet of each other. Even from this height, Steve could easily see the puncture wounds riddling their chests, weapons lying innocently at their sides.

Unlike other dreams, Steve wasn't the aggressor here. He was simply an observer. In fact, he felt very little for the dead men. They had done this to themselves. It was obvious that the humans were much more a danger to themselves than any animal could be.

He dropped down effortlessly from the high vantage point of the tree branch. He took another look around at the bodies strewn on the ground, and bounded off into the darkness.

***

For most of the residents in the town proper of Twin Lakes, the whole year of wild stories, legendary beasts roaming the woods and strange encounters was only a mild distraction from the everyday normalcy of life. Many people still considered the entire thing a myth, made up in the minds of a bunch of crazy folks. Others believed the legend served to cover up various crimes, some of which were rather violent. Still others felt the entire thing was a hoax, and still blamed the AML crew. Regardless of the assortment of popular beliefs, one thing was in common. The creature, if it did exist, was out in the depths of the state forest. Only a handful of folks at all had seen or heard it, and yes, there were a few more casualties than in a normal year. Those guys from Ohio got what they deserved, out shooting when it wasn't even hunting season yet. But again, it was a problem that was occurring in the woods, away from town and civilization.

That is, until the third weekend in October.

MaryAlice Whittle was walking her little fox terrier on the sidewalk in front of the public library when she first heard the howl. Generally, she got her exercise right around sunset, when the foot traffic was much slower and the sidewalks were clear. With the change in daylight saving time moving to the first week in November, there was still a little bit of daylight now at 6:05 pm. Though she was normally a power walker, cruising several laps around and through town, the noise caused her to completely stop in her tracks. The howl was long and drawn out, and couldn't have been more than a little outside of town. Even through the layers of warm clothing a chill ran up her spine. Her knees weakened, and it took all she had to stay standing upright. Her little dog Chelsey had gone on high alert. The fox terrier's ears were pointed straight up, the scruff on her back and neck was up, and her fangs were exposed. She had pulled tightly to the end of her leash, and was straining to be let loose upon her unseen enemy.

Chelsey let out a loud series of barks, unafraid of anything. But MaryAlice was scared. Her mind began recalling the various stories that passed around town, tales of a wolf-like creature with golden eyes and sharp fangs and claws. It could prowl like a canine and yet stand like a man. Her fear got the better of her, and she scooped up her little dog, double-timing it the remaining few blocks to home. The whole way home, Chelsey leaned up over her shoulder and barked off into the distance.

MaryAlice wasn't the only person to hear the Dogman. All around town, residents paused whatever they were doing and listened to the deep, guttural noise. No one could exactly point to where it came from, and if anyone were to ask around, everyone would have a different idea of its origin. Older folks rose up from their lawn chairs on their porches, listening intently while their hands shook. Kids playing catch froze in mid-step before hightailing it back to the safety of home. The golfers squeezing a last round on the public course before the season ended jumped in their carts and scuttled back to the clubhouse. At the SnappyCut, Clyde Miller, the local barber, paused as he was refinishing the cedar shingles on the front on his store. And in the parking lot of the village market, the few locals who preferred to shop near closing time to avoid the last throng of tourists and late-summer folk who packed the store all day long, rushed to the safety of their cars, some even forgetting the large bags of dog food and cat litter on the little wire shelf under their shopping cart. Suddenly, many in town found they needed to be at home right away.

While many people were out in the state forest armed to the teeth and looking for a chance to capitalize on the reward for the Dogman, the creature had left the rural countryside. Maybe it sought the safety and quietude of the town of Twin Lakes after all of the wild shooting. And perhaps it finally was finished with searching the woods and was ready to resume its endless pursuit in town. Regardless of the reason, the many town residents would soon be having their own sightings and encounters.

***

Chief Thompson was pulling another all-nighter. Since the two bloody incidents in the state forest, he'd been working more and more hours. Nearly every waking hour was spent on duty, either monitoring the station or patrolling the little town. His on-duty deputies were out scouring the woods, leaving him to run the office and take care of Twin Lakes proper. He vowed to work whatever hours were necessary to see this madness over and done with. It wasn't the first time he wished he were retired to some little village in the Upper Peninsula without a care in the world.

He'd already called on the state and county police, but to no avail. They still laughed at him and the whole situation. As far as they were concerned, it was some mass hysteria gone wild. Both groups that had died were out-of-towners, and they probably got what they deserved. The Ohio hunting party shot themselves up. And the group from Hollywood, well, anything could happen with those folks. They were probably doped up or something, and besides, they were trespassing in a very dangerous and unstable area. It's happened before, you betcha. Anything's possible when it comes to people from California. Michigan folks were generally glad they were a long distance from the West Coast.

The chief even tried the Governor's office again, but was directed to his county unit. That run-around didn't help one bit.

The local law enforcement would take the brunt of it all, good or bad. There was no cavalry to come in and save them.

And so it was that Chief Thompson was slumped over his desk filling out paperwork for his officers deep into the night. The long hours he was heaping on them, the least of all he could do was help with their paperwork. He was already on his umpteenth cup of coffee, and he'd stopped for far too many smoke breaks since he came in at noon. At least town was quiet. There were a few strange howls reported by folks, but no sightings or incidents. At least not for another half hour.

***

"Lefty" Cramer was what you might call the town drunk. He lived in a small rental cabin just off the river. His government disability paid for his rent, his meager foodstuffs, and even some of his booze. Lefty also collected bottles and cans to return for the deposit to make up for what the government wouldn't give him. He was a regular at the Moosehead Bar, at least when he had some cash to spare. Mostly he slept in all day, avoiding the bright sunlight, and then came out to prowl when it got started getting dark. He always hit the happy hours, and bounced from bar to bar getting in as many shells as he could at the lower prices. Then he'd typically settle down at whichever establishment he'd ended up at, head usually spinning, and sip a drink at the end of the bar, soaking up the atmosphere. Not many people ever talked to him, though most knew him, at least by sight. He was a regular fixture.

When the Moosehead finally booted him out at midnight, Lefty staggered out and down Canal Street toward home. His lanky five-nine frame was certainly a sight to see, shuffling along the edge of the dusty, potholed street. His home was only a few blocks from the trio of bars in downtown Twin Lakes. He could make it home blindfolded; most nights he might as well have been blindfolded. The only bad part of the trip was passing the rear of the police station. Sometimes the young officers hassled him as he was wobbling past. On nights when his senses were a bit more oriented, he'd walk a block around to avoid the township building. But this night, he was quite snookered, and wanted the quickest way home. But for some reason, not the alcohol, mind you, things didn't seem right this evening. The air was still and hot, and no one was about. Not that there were too many folks out and about on a Sunday night anyway. But it was just dead out here.

A loud crash scared Lefty so badly he nearly wet himself. He jumped backwards into the street, which was quite a feat in itself considering his condition, and swung his arms out in circles to balance himself so he wouldn't land on his bottom. He stared at the source of the sound: some metal trashcans on the side of a small garage were lying at various angles to each other, one lid still spinning to a standstill on the pavement. He continued staring at the little alley between the garage and the next little house. In the downtown area, the tiny houses, which were really only cabins, were basically piled on top of each other from the lake or river back toward the main street. Only thin patches of grass separated each cabin from the neighbor's. Of course, many houses made up for such close proximity by having river frontage, and that made even the meanest cabin worth its weight in gold.

Lefty blinked a few times, then shook his head in a vain attempt to clear his thoughts. He'd almost forgotten why he was looking in that direction. It must have been some critter, probably a 'coon or a skunk. That got him going again; he certainly didn't want to run into a skunk on the way home. He double-timed it, though his attempt at speed was more of a comical ambling. He was on the same block as the police station now, though he was going to chance an encounter with the young punk deputies rather than a potential skunking.

Another loud noise caused him to spin nearly around and face the left side of the street. Once again his hands went out to steady himself. At first his clouded mind didn't register the sound, but it came again quickly, and this time his eyes opened up in fear. It was the loud, low growl of some large animal. The corners of his mouth dropped open as he saw a pair of glowing yellow eyes staring back at him from the shadows between two cabins. He stopped and rubbed his eyes, not sure if he was truly seeing something or if he'd just had too many drinks this evening. The eyes were still there.

Lefty realized very quickly he was in a horrible predicament. He slowly began backing up, doing his best to control his fear. After a few steps, he turned and, still slowly, shuffled sideways down the street, half turned to watch the eyes. For a second he thought maybe he'd just move on his way and everything would be fine. That passed when he saw the eyes move out from between the cabins and slowly follow him.

He didn't run, he just stuck his hands in his pants pockets and kept shuffling along, though his pace was picking up every few seconds. He tried to whistle like nothing was wrong, but his mouth had gone dry. His body was sideways so he could watch his pursuer, those glowing eyes keeping pace, staying in the dark shadows that completely hid the rest of the animal's body.

A deep, resonating growl emanated from the darkness, and Lefty didn't need another clue to spur on his next action. He broke into a run, or at least the best version of a sprint one in his condition could muster, toward the only bright light on the street. As he neared the building, he realized it was the Twin Lakes police station, which under different circumstances he might do his best to avoid. But right now, it was sanctuary. Fifty feet away, 30 feet away, 10 feet away. Lefty had stopped looking back over his shoulder to focus all of his remaining concentration on reaching the safety of the station. He could hear the creature's footsteps pounding on the gravel shoulder of the street, the heavy panting of its raspy breath. Despite his spinning head, Lefty had the distinct impression the creature in the darkness was only playing with him, toying with him. It could take him any moment it wanted.

Almost out of nowhere, and certainly before he was ready for it, the door slammed against him, knocking the breath out of him. Actually, Lefty had run into the door, because he was listening to the creature behind him. His drunken state was compounded by the stars he was now seeing circle before his eyes because of the impact. However, just enough sanity was left to grasp the handle, yank the door open, and fall inside, pulling it tightly behind him.

Chief Thompson heard the ruckus in the vestibule, and pushed aside his paperwork to go see what was happening at the front door. The station was designed with a double locked entry way, creating a small secured room so all visitors could be screened before entering the office proper. Not that the little jail inside was ever filled enough with dangerous criminals who might have friends that would try to break them out. But security was paramount, especially in the current world of unpredictable violence.

The chief sauntered over to the safety glass window and looked out. Nothing. He couldn't have imagined the loud crash and bang of the outer door, and he certainly didn't hear it close again if someone had left. Then he looked down, and saw a body lying inert on the floor. The chief squinted his eyes, attempting to discern the situation before moving past the inner security door. The body still wasn't moving, but after a few seconds he was able to recognize it as belonging to Lefty Cramer. The Chief had had run-ins with Lefty over the years, as might be imagined. Despite Lefty's shoddy appearance and addictions, the chief knew him as a decent fellow. Lefty certainly never meant anybody any harm. That his body was lying comatose in the station vestibule was a shock and distress to the police chief.

The inner door opened as Chief Thompson quickly stepped into the little room. He bent over the motionless man, checking immediately for signs of life. Relief flooded the chief as he found a strong pulse, but revulsion hit him as he smelled the alcohol wafting off of Lefty as the man was pulled upright. Instantly, Lefty's eyes sprang open in fear, startling the chief, and the drunken man shook in a near convulsion, muttering something incoherent under his breath. The chief spoke softly and soothingly to Lefty, calming him down and reassuring him everything was okay.

"M-m-m-monster," sputtered Lefty continually between spasms. "Outs-s-s-ide." The chief had to strain to understand what he was saying, but as soon as it registered, the chief sprang into action. There was only one monster in this area that could scare a man nearly to death, and if it was truly right outside, the chief was going to dispose of it once and for all. No one, man or monster, was going to terrorize his little town, especially right outside his office.

He pulled closed the inner door, leaving Lefty to recover in the vestibule. For the first time in many years, the chief drew his sidearm and clicked off the safety. Though he did target practice often, it had been a long time since the weapon was drawn while on duty, and only the third time ever. He looked out the window of the outer door at the area flooded under the night light outside. Nothing was out of the ordinary. Pistol at the ready, he opened the door, stepped into the night and closed it tightly behind him

Chief Thompson pulled out his trusty (and heavy) service flashlight and clicked on the high-powered beam. Scouting from left to right, he moved along the edge of the sidewalk and the street still beneath the floodlight shining from the roof above. Nothing—no sight, no sound. He doubled back under the illuminated area, still shining his powerful flashlight into the darkness beyond.

When he was satisfied the immediate scene was secured, he backed up to the station door. Just as he was reaching to open it up, he heard for the first time the beastly growl echo across the town. It was a few blocks away by now, but it still sent chills right up the chief's spine. The sound was like nothing he'd ever heard before, and certainly belonged to no ordinary animal. The growl was far too ominous, too horrific, and too malevolent. Like some cartoon character, his knees began knocking, and he nearly fell backward against the door. He became a believer right then and there. This wasn't some nutcase running around. It wasn't mass hysteria. And it wasn't just some myth. There *was* something, some creature, some monster, terrorizing his town. And he had no idea how to stop it. He didn't know if it *could* be stopped.

CHAPTER 12

November 2007

The town of Twin Lakes is named for the two large lakes it is nestled between. However, it would be more aptly named Tri-Rivers, because the town itself is divided up between three large rivers that flow into and between Carson Lake and Long Lake. Three old and unique bridges, originally built of cement and stone by the CCC, offer the only passage across the various sections of town, separated by natural (and a few man-made) canals. The atypical land split by the water features forced a unique design found in no other town in northern Michigan. Properties had oddly shaped lots as every structure competed for the valuable water frontage. Other than the heavy concrete bridges, the limited-access freeway, which was yet another barrier to through traffic, offered the only alternate route through town, and that was an exit three miles north or an exit nine miles south. It could be absolutely horrendous when MDOT worked on any of the bridges. Luckily, this didn't occur too often.

The Walleye River's headwaters are quite a distance to the south, nearly 22 miles away. The current gathers strength and speed as it empties into Carson Lake right next to the State Park Campground. It is one of Michigan's fastest rivers, and a favorite among kayakers and canoeists. The Walleye River is also excellent for fishing. Upstream are trout and suckers, while bass, pike, and walleye tend to hang out at its mouth, drawing many locals in little fishing craft to drift at the south end of Carson Lake.

Connecting the pair of lakes is the Bear River, just over a mile long, which curves and twists right through the center of town. Cottages line its banks on both sides, some not more than little cabins and others large edifices to display wealth and affluence. The busiest of the three rivers, it empties Carson Lake and flows steadily into Long Lake. Dredged annually, it is easily wide enough to allow passage of boats up to 42 feet between the lakes. Hot weekends could see bumper to bumper traffic on the Bear.

The Crooked Creek empties the watershed of the state forest east of town and deposits it into Long Lake, just a quarter-mile up from the Bear River. Though truly just a creek way up in the woods near its headwaters, only a few feet deep and maybe a dozen or 15 feet across, Crooked Creek opens into a half-mile-wide marshy area at its mouth at the south end of Long Lake. This wetland of roughly a thousand acres is called "the Spreads" by the locals. It is an excellent site for pan fish and duck hunting, if you are strong enough to paddle a small rowboat through all of the thick reeds and grasses growing off the rich soil deposits. All winter, little wooded shanties mark the favorite fishing holes of hundreds of locals trying to bring in the prized monsters of the deep: pike, muskies, and sturgeon.

The flow of water eventually leaves Long Lake, running through the Cheboygan River and out into the cold depths of Lake Huron. Boaters could navigate this inland waterway from Lake Huron nearly to Lake Michigan, making it a desirable and famous route for pleasure cruising. Several marinas provide snacks and gas fill-ups, and a number of bars and restaurants offer docks for pull-up service. Boaters could spend all day on the water, eating, drinking, and enjoying the wonderful weather. With these easily-accessed points of refilling fuel for boats and humans alike, it was no surprise some folks even lived on their boats for days at a time.

The three rivers, along with the freeway, create several oddly triangular shapes of land that are geographically isolated from each other. The only way between the land masses are the bridges. The water itself becomes a natural dividing line, the curves and bends of the three rivers and the lakes' shorelines forming the backyards of many properties. Waterfront property is truly a valuable commodity in Twin Lakes, and everybody wants a piece of the action, whether it is for private homes or businesses.

***

November marks the real change of season from autumn to winter. Though in many years the real measurable snow won't arrive until December, the eleventh month brings with it the cold gusts of wind and the hard, violent storms down from Canada. The first snowfalls might occur in October or November, but they are generally short-lived, the once beautiful white coating on the ground turning to brown and gray mud within a few hours.

First snow usually tells the locals it's time to officially wind up the hoses, bring in the grill, cover the yard furniture, and otherwise batten down the yards and houses for winter.

By now, the regular hunting season was drawing in its usual share of sportsmen, though these folks were up north to hunt the normal game. They didn't come for the wild stories of huge rewards or monsters in the woods. They came for the bucks and does, the traditional Michigan big game. And they weren't disappointed. All of the traffic the state forest had seen over the past month and a half actually kept the deer moving much more regularly than they might normally have. Once the final tallies were done by the DNR, the 2007 deer harvest would be the best in recorded history.

First in were the bow hunters, followed two weeks later by the rifle hunters. With no reported signs of the beast in the state forest for weeks, most of the "big game" hunters returned home disappointed. The $50,000 reward remained unclaimed. And the normal, everyday hunters were able to fill all their permits easily.

**

Steve Nolan was staying in town for Thanksgiving weekend. School ended with a half-day on Wednesday, so he had some extra time to lay on the couch and relax from the stress of classes. He loved the kids, sure, but everyone needed a break from each other, especially this time of year.

Daylight changed over to night in the span of a few minutes, as it will in the late autumn. Steve was flipping through the channels and gnawing on a slice of cold pizza. Accidentally, he knocked over his soda, and was forced to jump into action, clearing everything off the coffee table. Beneath the pile of junk mail and several magazines was the weathered, old journal Markus had given him when they parted in September. It stared up at him, almost begging to be read. On an impulse, he picked it up. He'd thought little of the book, and had absently tossed it there when he came home depressed from the entire AML incident. It was a lucky thing he'd been forced to go through everything when he spilled the soda, or the diary could have been lost to history yet again.

Steve initially leafed absently through the little journal. But after a few moments, he was captivated by the personal narrative written in ancient pen and ink. He flipped back to the first page and read each scripted word with care. His eyes widened with understanding as each fragile page was turned. His fingers began to shake, first little quivers that eventually led to more major shudders. His teeth bit slightly into lips. The expedition. The burial mound. The ghostly image that became real. The trading of the other gemstones to villagers along a path north to the fort at Mackinac. Settling down and raising a family, despite the awful nightmares. Generations of descendants living in the northern tip of the peninsula. Steve's family.

The nightmares. They were eerily similar to those Steve endured all year. Scenes of running through the wild lands at night. Encounters where the old frontiersman actually thought he was the creature. The incident at the burial mound, only he could see himself, frightened, through the beast's eyes.

And on the last page, a drawing, a sketch of the original necklace as it was remembered before the gems were detached, one by one, and passed along. Seeing that drawing wrapped it all up. All the puzzle pieces were now in place.

Sitting bolt-upright, Steve removed the little necklace and carefully examined the sharp-ended black jewel with the spider-webbed red veins. His jaw dropped. It might be comical in some other situation, but certainly not here. Not only did it resemble the gem from the journal, but it was an exact match. This *was* one of the cursed treasures stolen from the sacred burial mound. It had to be. It all made so much sense now. His dreams. His connection to the beast. Feeling the search in his dreams. He wasn't the creature; the creature was searching for him!

All of the sightings over the years. The creature was reclaiming its own. It was tracking the gems down, each and every one, following the trail northward. The incidents the AML research team had found were of the beast recovering its precious treasure. The yearly sightings must have ended when the creature found the next piece of the necklace. The poor folks who'd been injured or killed were only in the way. And Steve was next.

The creature was coming for him, for the gemstone he wore around his neck.

How could he not have seen it before? How could he have been so clueless? It all seemed so obvious now. Maybe he'd known, deep down all along, and his subconscious had kept it buried. It didn't matter now. Steve ran his fingers through his dark red hair. He knew right then and there what he had to do. He had to return the gemstone. It was the only way to stop the Dogman from terrorizing the town. It was the only way to stop any further bloodshed.

The little clock on the microwave blinked at 8:37. Steve didn't care about the time. This couldn't wait. He'd drive around, all night if need be, until he forced an encounter to occur.

He slipped on his boots and zipped up his black fleece jacket. He'd do what was right, right now. He'd find the creature, this night, and give it back the gemstone. It wasn't a family heirloom any longer. It was a symbol of death.

Steve hoped it would stop his horrific dreams. And he prayed, not for the last time, that he'd make it out of this whole affair alive.

***

Steve knew the creature had been prowling around town after so many months out in the wilderness. Plenty of townspeople had heard it at night, and there were a few sightings that could be considered reputable. Steve knew it had come here for him, for his gemstone, and it would search through every building, every home, and every person until it found the heirloom.

Though it was only nearing nine o'clock, the night was extremely dark and Steve vaguely remembered it was a new moon, so the only bright lights in the gloom would be from homes and the occasional vehicle. Little pinpricks of stars were scattered overhead in the clear firmament, and it was easy to see the dark shadows of trees and buildings standing out against the black sky.

He gassed up before the last store in town closed its doors for the evening. With so few actual full-time residents and all the multitudes gone back south for the winter, most establishments closed up shop at nine or earlier. Steve fired up the little truck, and began his vigilant cruise through town. He'd methodically navigate the little back streets of each section of town before traversing a stone bridge to the next neighborhoods. Nearly all of the cabins and cottages were dark and boarded up for the winter. Most of the residents couldn't afford to live down here near the water anyway.

He'd made several revolutions around the many winding streets and crossed out the middle land section, called "downtown" by the townsfolk, when his headlights caught something, some sort of large shadow disappear around the side of the Twin Lakes Diner. Immediately he swung into the parking lot.

The vehicle picked up speed as Steve's adrenaline began to run.

The diner had closed for the evening at seven o'clock, and the staff typically locked up just after 8:30 when all was cleaned and ready for the coffee crowd the following morning. Now at 10:30, it was deserted.

Steve turned left around the back of the diner, past the pair of large, green garbage dumpsters and there it was. The creature that had terrorized the entire area. The beast that was searching for him. The Dogman. It was right there! But Steve had been going far too fast, and the creature wasn't about to budge.

It was his first true face-to-face encounter with the Dogman. And though it lasted only a split second, Steve took in all its features, just as if time had slowed down for a portrait to form in his mind. It was up walking on its powerful hind legs, and had just turned to face Steve's little truck. Its black, hairy chest was wide, muscles rippling just under the fur. A paw/hand was rising up to block the truck's headlights, long claws casting pointed shadows across its neck. The creature's muzzle was open, a growl emerging between its fangs that were dripping with saliva. The Dogman's face was indeed a mix of canine and human; it was shaped like that of a great dog or wolf, and yet it took on a far too human expression of surprise.

Steve's little red truck smashed into the creature, denting in the front grille and chrome bumper. The impact also sent Steve's metal toolbox exploding out the windshield, tools and broken shards of glass flying in all directions. The Dogman suffered damage too, being blasted backward nearly 20 feet, tumbling off into the parking lot. Adding insult to injury, the creature was peppered by a multitude of wrenches, screwdrivers, and pliers.

The crash completely caught Steve off guard. Instinctively, he slammed on the brakes, locking the wheels as his right foot held the pedal fast to the floor of the truck. His forehead slammed against the worn steering wheel, raising a red welt and spinning his mind for a few seconds.

Unfortunately, it was the beast that recovered first. It shivered a bit in the cold November night, testing all of its faculties as it turned toward the stationary vehicle. Ever so slowly, it strode toward Steve's truck, the pair of headlights slightly blinding it from seeing inside the cab. It continued forward with the slightest limp until it could peer in above the lights directly at the driver.

Recognition flashed through the creature's glowing eyes as it spied the necklace around Steve's neck. It had bounded loose from inside Steve's collar in the accident, and now lay in plain sight, pinched up around his chin. Steve shook off the pain of the accident, carefully feeling and rubbing his jaw with his right hand to see if anything was broken. His fingers moved up to the knot forming on his forehead. He pulled the necklace back down, and suddenly remembered what he had hit that had caused all of this damage. He looked up to see the Dogman rise to its full height, the bulk of its furry body bathed in the headlights. The little tendrils of its hair rippled in the light breeze. Steve's eyes widened as he realized he was staring over his steering wheel at the embodiment of grim death.

His original intent of returning the gemstone to the beast was buried far beneath the immediate fear and survival instincts. At this moment, Steve could think of nothing but escape, getting as far away as possible from the horror in his headlights.

He threw the truck in reverse, finally lifting his foot from the brake, and slammed down on the gas pedal. The little truck jumped and dashed backward through the parking lot. Steve had no idea where he was going, just so long as he was heading away from the creature. He watched through the windshield as it loped after him, and he never saw the trailer of canoes situated at the end of the parking lot 10 feet up from the hidden river below. The little truck, heading into its final stretch of usefulness, barreled into the trailer, spilling a dozen aluminum canoes in all directions, including down the embankment to the Walleye River. Rather than slide down the slope, Steve's truck went right over, catching air as it hung in the evening darkness suspended over the wide river. After what seemed an eternity to Steve, who had only enough time to realize where he'd sent his truck, the vehicle plunged tailgate-fist into the icy water.

The truck was sinking fast into the depths of the river, even though the strong current continued to push it toward Carson Lake. The impact with the river jarred Steve for the second time this evening, and he had just enough time to scramble out through the broken windshield as the truck's cab slipped under the water, followed a few seconds later by the hood. Steve was practically blind, splashing in the water and scared out of his wits. Only a little light emanated from the parking lot above. He knew at any moment the Dogman would launch itself at him and it would be all over. But the first thing was to keep from drowning. Enough light drifted down to him to spy a canoe floating downstream a few feet away, not too far from the opposite bank. He reached its back end, grasping the gunwales to keep his head above the water while his feet kept kicking to propel him further and faster downstream.

Like a phantasm from a horrible dream, the dim light up at the top of the river bank was eclipsed by the blackness of the snarling, growling Dogman as it launched itself high into the air, arms and legs spread, claws and fangs bared in the anticipation of catching its prey unaware. Luckily the river was a good 60 feet across at this point, just a few hundred yards from Carson Lake. The creature, though it did sail through the cold air, landed with a tremendous belly-smacker, spraying water and rippling waves in all directions as it submerged. Only moments later it resurfaced, shook the water from its head and muzzle, and began to paddle after Steve.

Steve was a pretty good swimmer, and now his life depended on the skill he'd first learned as a child. He ignored the numbness in his legs from the icy water and the heaviness of his soaked jeans and fleece jacket as they tried to pull him downward into the depths. Adrenaline kept him going. He propelled himself forward with great kicks of his tired legs. The canoe cut the water a bit for him, enabling him to outdistance his pursuer just a bit.

The creature wasn't a fast swimmer, but it kept coming after him.

Steve knew he couldn't last much longer in the cold water, so he steered the canoe to the near bank. He emerged quickly, letting the canoe drift down to Carson Lake, and scrambled the best he could up the slippery dirt slope. More than once did his feet slide on the muddy ground, and he panicked each time. The creature was a good 20 yards behind him in the river, and moving fairly slowly, but he needed to put some real distance between it and himself immediately. He needed a place of sanctuary, some place he could hide out. What he really needed was a place he could lock himself in where the creature couldn't reach him. As he ran, terrified, his eyes darted around him, searching the few lights of town for a suitable place.

But it wasn't the few lights still on in town at this time of night that caught his attention. Rather, it was a location with a lack of lights, a large, completely dark structure he headed toward with all the strength he could muster down to his shivering legs.

***

Though progress occurs slowly in Twin Lakes, the community has gone through some changes throughout its history. Sometimes these transformations are measured in the span of years or decades rather than days or months. Despite technological and social progress that occurs in other parts of the state and across the country, many things remained the same in Twin Lakes as they were 20, 30 or even 50 years ago.

The biggest change of 2001 was the relocation of Carson Lake Marina's Showroom and boat storage from lakeside to a larger, more elaborate structure south of town. The new building, a monstrous edifice, stands proudly on the corner of state highways 64 and 29. It has three times the floor space of the previous building for showcasing the latest boat models, plus brand new pole barns tucked in the rear of the wooded lot for plenty of storage.

The previous building down on Lake Street sits at the water's edge of the downtown strip, less than 50 yards from where the Walleye River empties into Carson Lake. It is now abandoned and awaiting its eventual demolition, yet still overlooks the marina slips where fancy boats of all sizes moor up in the summer months. The marina executives have yet to decide the building's fate, yet they fully know the 10 acres of land it sits up on are perhaps the most desirable bits of property on either of the two lakes. Though the building is still used for deep storage of items that won't be missed while they're collecting layers of dust, the 48 boat slips immediately outside continue to be heavily used every year from May to September. However, now in November, the entire site is vacant. All services have been moved up to the new building for the winter months.

The old marina showroom, though not as substantial or modern as its new successor, is still the largest structure located on Carson Lake itself. And being completely abandoned, it is an absolute black space, an empty hole among the little lights of buildings and homes surrounding it.

Steve thought it might be his best shot at hiding out from the creature. An abandoned, empty building would be perfect, and it was right here. There really wasn't any other place to go. He was exhausted, tired from the flight. His body was responding and running on pure will power now.

Twenty feet from the building, he paused, listening to the quietude of the night and planning his next move. The stars were indeed bright down by the water's edge, since hardly any lights were on in the many crowded cottages and cabins that were only inhabited during the summer months. A light breeze wafted across the expanse of Carson Lake. Sweat mixed with the cold river water dripped down his face, arms, and torso, and its evaporation from his bare, goose-pimpled skin chilled him right down to the bone. Steve shivered, a long, jerking spasm that started at his neck and shoulders and ran all the way to his lower legs. He wasn't sure he could last much longer out here in the cold night. If the creature didn't get him, he just might freeze to death!

He couldn't lead the creature to any further human contact, for fear of what it might do to someone who got in its way. That would keep him from any place with lights. The marina was a dark place to conceal himself, rest in safety, and retain at least a little body heat. He needed only to find a way in.

***

Breaking into the old marina building set off the silent alarm, a blinking code light on a console several hundred miles away in the safe confines of a security corporation. The on-duty technician took several moments to locate the proper customer in the computer files since that particular code had never been triggered before. Upon finding the information, he made two phone calls, one to the president of the Carson Lake Marina and a second to the Twin Lakes Police Department.

Exactly in the same position as he'd been over the previous nights for nearly two months now, Chief Thompson was sitting at his little desk, smoking Camels, drinking the black sludge he called coffee, and filling out paperwork. In the past few weeks, he'd been on several wild goose chases, responding to sightings and occurrences all over town. Luckily none had included physical interactions with the creature, and he was sure some were just stories based on the wild imaginations of the scared townspeople. He firmly believed the town's enacted curfew helped curtail the number of possible meetings between human and beast.

But somewhere out there, the chief knew the creature was roaming around his town. He was a bit startled by the phone ringing, and looked over at the little digital clock. It read 11:03, which might just be about right for another sighting. The chief was mildly surprised (and even somewhat pleased) at the call from the security company. At least it wasn't another creature disturbance.

That's what he prayed as he left the office and headed for his patrol car. Maybe it'd be just a normal, run-of-the-mill break-in he could easily handle. He wasn't sure he'd know what to do if or when he did encounter the creature.

***

Steve had crouched down and hidden himself beneath the pontoons of a deck boat that had been abandoned inside the old marina building. Of the several boats in disrepair on the former showroom floor, this large pontoon gave him the best chance of concealment. He hoped his footprints in the dust that coated the cement wouldn't betray him. He had a fairly clear line of sight to the side door he'd battered his way through. Once broken, it wouldn't close tightly again, and it swung freely a few inches from the door jamb.

Still out of breath, Steve had only a few precious seconds to screen himself and lie silently on the dirty cement floor before he heard the scratching of the creature's claws on the wooden door. It was a harsh, grating sound, like fingernails on a chalkboard when Steve was a young student in elementary school. Though his lungs were burning, he held his breath, making absolutely no noise, looking out as the Dogman pushed open the door and, on its back two powerful legs, stepped into the building.

The beast paused, sniffing the air. Though dark outside, it was nearly total blackness in the building. Steve could see the creature's outline in the doorway, though it couldn't see the disturbed dust of his prints as they disappeared under the boat. Steve was down on his belly, the pontoons only giving about two feet of space from the floor to the deck. If the creature did want him, it would have to crawl down here too, and that would give Steve a small bit of time to scramble out the back, since the outboard motor had long been removed.

The Dogman began its thorough search through the darkened building. It continued to sniff the air, long, deep breaths that would eventually unveil Steve's position. It strode carefully and purposefully, toe claws clicking on the cement floor with each step. Though it left the direct line of sight out the front of the pontoons, Steve could track it by the creature's footsteps and by its breathing. It had exerted itself too in the wild chase.

Steve's mind was a complete jumble and he was nearly ready to crack. He tried to breathe as silently as possible, reminding himself it was death to be heard. Of course, his heart was still racing, and his nerves were doing their best to try and shake his hands and limbs. It was a matter of will to keep his body under control. Part of his mind kept telling him he was dead, he'd die, it would just be a matter of time. Another part demanded survival. He could do this, just lie still and things would be okay. Yet another part of him wanted to actually confront the creature, to lay it all on the line.

After a few moments of getting his thoughts settled, Steve noticed he'd lost track of the creature. That was a huge mistake on his part. He listened intently, closing his eyes, straining himself to shut off all distracting noises in an effort to locate the Dogman. It was gone. The abandoned building was dead quiet. Steve didn't move a muscle. It could be right there waiting for him to shift, to give himself away. He wouldn't do it, he wouldn't expose himself. He'd force himself to wait, however long it took.

Steve jumped, if that was even possible in the little confined space as a long, nasty growl emanated from behind him, from the rear of the little boat where once an outboard motor had been attached. He looked back and saw it, the Dogman, squatted down on all fours, trying to squeeze itself under the boat. It was much bigger than Steve in its muscular upper body, and it had a hard time pushing past the motor mount and crawling between the pontoons. But it would force itself through, nonetheless, in a few seconds. Steve screamed back, startled by the creature's appearance, and immediately began crawling forward with all speed he could muster, staying just out of reach of the Dogman's long arms and claws.

Though Steve had a few feet lead, and the Dogman was still battering its way through the rear of the pontoon, it would still be a close call to escape. Steve's adrenaline was pumping as he emerged from under the boat. He tried to get up and sprint for the door, but the dust and grime on the floor, now mixed with the dripping water from human and animal, was a slippery slime that provided no traction. Steve slid ahead, losing balance as his upper body toppled downward and his feet shot out behind. But he did have enough momentum to glide all the way to the wall, where he crashed into a pile of loose odds and ends. A few feet to his left was the door outside, his escape, and yet the collision had left him nearly senseless. He couldn't have run outside if he wanted to at this moment. His jaw had hit the cement floor during the fall, and the impact had rattled his brain. The pile of junk gave him small nicks and cuts all over from the various sharp objects he'd run into.

The growling and howling continued as the Dogman neared the front edge of the pontoon. It had spied its quarry just feet ahead of him. It prepared to leap as it materialized from the under the boat.

It never had the opportunity to go airborne. Several thunderous booms echoed through the building, hurting Steve's ears to no end. The bullets had hit the Dogman in the chest and shoulders, pummeling it backward so that its knees bent over the front deck of the pontoon, causing it to fall over.

Chief Thompson had pulled the trigger seven times, unloading every bullet in the clip of his Glock 45. He wasn't about to make the mistake of letting the creature escape. He was going to end it all right here and now.

He'd just pulled up, surveyed the scene, cautiously approached the busted door, and heard the crash and loud growling. Sidearm drawn, he stepped into the doorway and there saw the stuff nightmares are made of. The creature, a mass of fur, fangs, claws, and eerie glowing yellow eyes, was a perfect target only a few feet away. The chief didn't even hesitate.

When the ringing in his ears finally subsided, Steve was able to look up and around. Seeing the chief, he smiled goofily, obviously out of sorts from the concussion he was now experiencing. The world steadied as Chief Thompson helped him to his feet. The two shared a brief moment of repose, and even in the darkness, each could see the other smile a little.

Suddenly the chief lurched forward, grunting as the air escaped his body in a mad rush. He fell to his knees on the hard cement, knocked forward by the blow from the Dogman's powerful forearm and hand. It wasn't dead! Steve fell as well, rolling to a ball just in front of the doorway. He looked up to see the Dogman standing over him, fangs bared, eyes glowing nastily down at him.

There was only one chance, one shot at salvation. He'd finally remembered why he'd left the comfort of his apartment in the first place this evening. He could only offer up the necklace, his family heirloom, in the hopes it was truly what the creature was searching for. If he was wrong, it wouldn't matter anyway. There was no means of escape. He couldn't keep running. He was out of breath and out of energy. The creature had taken seven slugs at point blank range, and they didn't even faze it. Steve could offer no further resistance to the Dogman. If it wanted him, so be it.

Everything pointed to the jewel that now glowed in a supernatural light. Steve bet the farm on this one. There were no other options.

Steve slipped the jeweled necklace up over his head and carefully placed it on the cement slab floor. Slowly, cautiously, he crawled away from the beast. Its eyes, once locked on him, now dropped to the jewel. It growled again, though with less menace this time. The creature lithely moved forward, and its tall lanky frame gracefully bent and scooped up the necklace.

Suddenly, the beast rose to its full height, easily towering a head or two over Steve if he'd been standing himself, and lifted its jaws to the ceiling, puffed its chest, and roared into the darkness of the night. It was the most awful sound Steve had ever heard, and from this close distance, he could even feel the force of the air blasting past him, almost through him. The roar echoed for many seconds through the marina building, reverberating off the boats in storage. Steve crouched, falling over on his side, certain that his time had now come, even though he'd returned the cursed jewel. He'd done what was needed, and yet now he'd still have to die. His last thought was that hopefully his sacrifice might save others later. His hands instinctively covered his face as he saw the creature rock on its haunches and spring through the frigid air at him.

Steve rolled over backward, anticipating the crushing blow, the sharp fangs, the stench of rotting flesh. But the impact never came; the creature had simply bounded right over his inert form and disappeared out the door into the darkness of the night.

***

December came and went with no sightings of the creature.

It was as if it had never existed, or had been a mass hallucination of the people of Twin Lakes. The county and state police departments gloated over the whole situation. They'd never let Chief Thompson forget it. He took much of the ribbing, knowing that they'd never believe him even if he did describe his last encounter. But a few people in the town knew the truth. They might not ever discuss it again, but the memories would be with them the rest of their lives.

Within a week of the final incident at the marina, Chief Thompson had his paperwork filled out and filed for retirement. Twin Lakes would have a new police chief as of January 1st, 2008.

Steve's nightmares stopped abruptly too. He slept so soundly every night for a week that at first he didn't even notice he wasn't having them. Once he did remember, he was afraid they would return, but his sleep wasn't interrupted by them again.

What little footage and sound bites that existed from the *American Myths & Legends* show made their way to various internet sites. These were all unsubstantiated by the show's producers, who couldn't find the source of the leak at their offices.

Douglas Wilson's conversion van collected a heavy covering of snow in the back corner of the police station parking lot. There was little response from the novelist's agents back in the city. In New York, there were other concerns than a missing novelist. If someone wanted to disappear, especially with the amount of money Wilson had amassed in his successful career, it was certainly his prerogative to do so. No one knew if he'd just given up writing or retired and left the public eye.

Apparently he wanted to be left alone. In the big city, what was one missing writer?

***

Christmas break had arrived, and Steve was extremely glad for the two-week break from school. He was checking his email one final time before the five-hour trip to Stambaugh, and one message among the loads of spam caught his attention. It was from Chad Russell. Steve hadn't spoken to those guys in months, and it had been weeks since he'd thought of them. Last he'd heard the three USC boys had split and each was working in a different TV venue. Despite the horrendous finish to the show, their resumés were impressive enough to get them through some doors that were normally closed to those at entry-level.

In show business, that was quite an accomplishment.

They were also quasi-celebrities on the internet.

Chad's email was brief, to the point, just the way he always conversed:

Dude, just checking to see if you're still there. All the posts from Twin Lakes have stopped. Did the Dogman check out? Is it gone? Write back if you're still alive. Chad.

Steve began clicking away on the keyboard of his laptop, smiling. He'd fire this last email away before heading north.

It's been taken care of, at least for this year, hopefully this decade. You were right, it was after something. Once it regained its lost property, it completely disappeared. Vanished! And tell Markus he was right too—the journal proved to be the key to it all. Take care, and best of luck. C/ya online. Steve

"I guess we'll find out in 10 years," Steve laughed, trying to be nonchalant, trying to convince himself as he said it aloud. However, he felt in his heart that the beast would continue to roam the north woods for a long time to come. If the story of his family heirloom, the cursed gemstone necklace, along with Chad's prediction of the creature's northward migration were indeed true, then there were other treasures the beast would undoubtedly be searching for in the area north of Twin Lakes in a little less than a decade.

An excerpt from
The Light

The Paulding Light has been a well documented phenomenon for decades, even centuries if one were to trace back all of the stories and legends. Even modern science had yet to explain it, though many folks tried their best to bend their explanations around the unusual occurrence.

Every night from dusk until dawn, regardless of the date, regardless of the weather, even regardless of the number of folks who might be watching, the light appears on the horizon, deep in the wilderness. It seems far too familiar of a sight, like a piece of human technology we all know and have seen before. It seems that we could explain it with any one of several causes. And yet it remains a mystery. Scientists from the nearby universities have studied it for decades with no further explanation. It is not something we have created.

The Paulding region in Michigan's Upper Peninsula is one of those 'thin' areas in the world, a place where ancient and unexplained powers still directed the course of nature. Native Americans, Celts, and even the Ancient Greeks among many other cultures in history, though millennia apart, shared similar beliefs of such places of power in the world. Stonehenge, Delphi, Giza, and even Atlantis were but the more commonly known and remembered locations. These were spots where the gods themselves interacted with human civilization.

This place held neither a power of good and evil, nor of positive and negative like some sort of natural magnet. Perhaps the Chinese had it closest with the concept of Yin and Yang, with every force in the universe having an opposing force to counterbalance it.

But truly, the light was just the harbinger of the greater power that existed deep in the dense, primeval forest. Again, it was neither a power of good nor of evil. It was a force that could give as well as demand, and it needed to do both to maintain its existence. And so, just as it could grant life, it needed to take life just as often...

***

The sun had set below the tree line to the left of the turnout, and its rays strained to reach over the deep expanse of the national forest. The very tops of the dense fir trees, towering fifty or sixty feet above, glistened in the diminishing sunlight, a stark contrast to the darkness at the forest floor. Visibility at ground level was only a few yards as the wide evergreen branches blocked nearly all penetration into the primeval woods. The gravel road, turnout, and power line were in shadow, though they wouldn't be truly dark for yet a half hour.

Skeeter pointed down the sandy trail of the power line where it met the horizon far to the northwest. A bright globe of light had appeared as if from over the hill that seemed a little more than a mile away.

"There it is, my man." The glowing orb shone brightly as it appeared to very slowly descend down the hill, following the massive steel towers holding up the long, drooping yet graceful curves of the electric cables. The little glowing dot was slightly bigger than a star you might see on a dark night far away from the light pollution of civilization, and yet from this distance it wasn't quite as large as the moon appeared to the naked eye. If you held your hand out at arms length, your pinkie finger could just hide it from sight.

"Yeah, right," Jason replied, not truly impressed. "That's a car's headlights from the other side."

Skeeter continued on patiently, knowing that was always the first response. "This road don't connect to anything. It's blocked off five miles up the trail, just like right here."

A large, steep hill of sand stretched across the trail. For added measure, a steel highway guard rail kept all traffic from traveling down the power line. There was no way a vehicle could get around it, at least not here at this end.

"Then someone's gone around the blockade. That's just some dude's brights flashing over the hill."

Skeeter was ready for such skepticism. He reached into his old leather satchel draped around his shoulder and pulled out a hand-held video camera.

"Ok, smart guy, you look through the view finder."

Jason opened the little swivel screen up to his eyes, zooming in as the autofocus brought in the power line clearly. He followed the line from tower to tower until the eerie light came into view. Jason stopped breathing for a few moments. He lowered the camera slightly, then brought it right back up.

"That camera has an 800x digital zoom. It'll bring you right up into the action. Tell me if you're not convinced," Skeeter said calmly. He'd obviously been through this ritual before.

It was one distinct ball of light, not two like from a pair of headlights. And even more strangely, it was changing colors. It faded from a bright white with almost a bluish tint to a yellow, an orange, and even a red. Then it cycled back again.

"If we could get a pair of cell phones, a GPS unit maybe..." Jason whispered slowly.

"Don't you think we'd have already tried those things?" countered Skeeter, looking plaintively at his friend. "I mean, I know we're just back-woods red-necks up here, but give us a little credit. It isn't the lights of the highway, it's not some cars two-tracking down the trail, and it's not a house or tower. There aren't any structures up that way. Believe you me, me and the boys've been all over every inch of that trail, and there just isn't any reason for that light to exist."

Jason smacked a mosquito on the right side of his neck. He watched as the light dimmed, fading to a tiny bright red speck, and then disappeared. Skeeter continued his litany.

"No one knows what it's for, where it comes from. I've lived here all my life, and I've seen it far too many times to count. But I'm telling you right now, something 'bout that light ain't right. It don't belong to this world. It gives me chills every time I see it."

***

Watch for *The Light* in 2008.

For more information, check out our website at:

http://www.mythmichigan.com